MW01488144

Where's the Rest of the Body?

A Joel Franklin Mystery, Volume 2

Ron Finch

Published by Ron Finch, 2018.

This is a work of fiction. Similarities to real people, places, or events are entirely coincidental.

WHERE'S THE REST OF THE BODY?

First edition. October 17, 2018.

Written by Ron Finch.

Dedication

This book, the second in a series of books revolving around my main character Joel Franklin, is dedicated to the few devoted readers, friends, and relatives who have made the mistake of asking me about my writing.

I am not reluctant to reply enthusiastically to their questions. I learn so much in writing each book that I find it hard to resist sharing what I've learned with anyone who is foolish enough to ask me "how's it going?" Not only are the books an exercise in improving as an author, they're also an opportunity for me to explore many tangents (via the Internet) as ideas pop into my head.

So, friends and relatives, this book is dedicated to you. Your interest in what I'm writing just adds fuel to the fire.

Books by Ron Finch

THE JOEL FRANKLIN MYSTERY Series:

Lightning at 200 Durham Street
Where's the Rest of the Body?

Important Quotes

"There are more things in heaven and earth, Horatio, than are dreamt of in your philosophy."

William Shakespeare

"Listen!"
Everyone's mother

"Believe nothing you hear, and only one half that you see."
Edgar Allen Poe

"Don't believe everything you think."
Allan Lokos

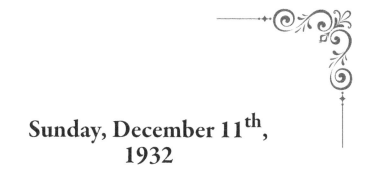

Sunday, December 11th, 1932

IT WAS A COLD DAY, but it wasn't too cold to go for a skate.

I was going with my friends, Jay, Georgie, and Sylvia. We were going to Sylvia's parents', the Graysons, who lived on the edge of town in a good-size home on a large half-acre lot. There were empty fields behind the house that collected water when it rained. Snow had come early this year, then there had been a short warm spell just at the start of December followed by very cold weather. As a result, there was a natural skating rink in the field behind Sylvia's parents' house.

Sylvia Grayson and Jay Jarvis had been married a little over two years earlier, in the summer of 1930. Times were tough, but who really thought they might get worse? It was a great wedding and everyone had had a good time that day. I was the best man and the master of ceremonies. It was my opportunity to tease Jay and I did so enjoyably. Jay usually got the better of me in our verbal dustups, but that day, as the master of ceremonies, I had had my way.

Since then, Jay and Sylvia have been through some hard times. Jay and his dad had had a small construction company, Jarvis Construction, but with the depression, and the unemployment rate in Canada around 27%, no one was building homes, farm outbuildings, or doing major home repairs. Like a lot of small companies, Jarvis Construction reached a point where they could no longer purchase supplies and they had had to shut down. This happened in the fall of 1930. With no money coming in, Sylvia and Jay had had to move in with Sylvia's

3

parents. But their life had brightened a little with the birth of their son Brad – named after Jay's dad – in mid-September 1931.

Despite the economic downturn, my mom and dad had so far managed to survive the depression. They were very fortunate. My mother's mom, Granny Watson, had come to live with my parents in the fall of 1930, after my grandpa died. Though she would be 70 on her birthday, she was still very active and a big help around the house, especially when it came to keeping track of my brother Ralph and my sister Emmylou. With the sale of the farm, granny was able to help my parents pay off the mortgage on their home. There was still a mortgage on the store, but it wasn't much, and compared to most people our family was very fortunate. There was so much hardship and so many people unemployed and so many people needing help that just getting from one day to the next was an accomplishment.

I had graduated from the University of Western Ontario in the spring of 1932. It made my mother proud. My dad was pleased too. Somehow or other, between me finding whatever work I could, and my parents scrimping, enough money was rounded up to get me to graduation. According to the 1932 Census, less than 3% of Canadians attended university, but I now had a BA in Business Administration. It sounded nice, but I was just as unemployed as everyone else.

I spent three months looking for some kind of employment relevant to the degree I had obtained. After a fruitless search, I realized that the best job I could get would be in my parents' corner store, Franklin's Groceries. But I wouldn't accept any money and they couldn't afford to pay me. I was getting free room and board at the store, though, so I guess I was the store's security guard. I had moved out of the family home in 1929 to go to UWO, and since then I had spent most of my time in London, even during the summer. Then, of course, in the fall of 1930, Granny Watson had inherited my room at 200 Durham Street.

Georgie and I were still the best of friends. But as I was unemployed, and times were tough, we decided to wait for a year or two to marry. That didn't mean we couldn't enjoy each other's company, though, so today I was going to have a good time. This afternoon the four of us were going to go skating while Sylvia's mom, Clara, babysat little Brad.

THE NATURAL RINK IN the field was good but it was far from perfect. In a couple places, there were bits of plowed earth that showed through the surface. Those patches were brown and easy to spot against the much lighter-colored snow and ice, but if you didn't see those brown patches you came to a quick stop and took a hard, unexpected seat on the rink.

We had a good time. A lot of exercise, fresh air, and tumbles. It wasn't bitterly cold, so we were comfortably warm in our toques, scarves, and knitted winter jackets. Just as we were getting ready to head back to the Grayson home for some hot chocolate and to admire baby Brad, Jay said:

"Joel, come over here and take a look."

I came to a stop beside Jay and looked in the direction he was pointing.

"See that large brown patch of earth showing through the ice? It's about 25 or 30 feet away."

I nodded.

"There's something in the middle of that brown patch," said Jay.

"I think it's just another chunk of earth," I said.

"You better take another look. It's not quite the same colour as the earth and it has a distinctive shape. It almost looks like an arm to me." Jay hollered at Sylvia and Georgie. "Why don't you two go back to the house and play with the baby until we get there. Clara will be glad to see you. Joel and I are going across part of the field to take a look at something. We won't be long."

When we got to the object that Jay had spotted, I bent over and picked it up. It was a neatly severed arm. We both almost gagged when we recognized what it was. I dropped it immediately.

"I'm afraid to look any further," said Jay.

"I don't think I should have picked it up," I said. "I just didn't realize what it was soon enough."

"It's time for the police," said Jay.

We quickly headed back to the Graysons' house.

As soon as we came through the back door we heard the happy babble of three women and one small child. The moment the women got a look at our faces, though, they knew something was seriously wrong.

"What's going on?" said Georgie. "What did you find?"

"There's no easy way to say this," said Jay. "We found somebody's arm. But we don't know where the rest of the body is."

"Oh my goodness!" yelped Clara.

Georgie and Sylvia turned pale. Baby Brad kept babbling. He was safe in Sylvia's arms.

"I need to use your phone. Right now," I said. "I have to call the police."

"Of course," said Clara, showing me the way.

"Police Station, Cst. Smith speaking," said a voice from the other end when they picked up. "How can I help you?"

"We were out skating this afternoon and found an arm," I said, my voice shaking.

"I don't think I understand what you're trying to tell me," said Cst. Smith, an irritable tone in his voice. "This isn't a prank, is it? If it is, it will get you in trouble. You can't be wasting my time."

"I'm sorry Cst. Smith, I didn't explain the situation very well. It's Joel Franklin phoning. We were skating this afternoon on the farm behind the Grayson house when we noticed something in the field. Jay Jarvis and I went over to get a closer look and saw that it was a human arm. It's been severed from someone's body. There is no sign of any other body parts nearby."

"Heaven help us," was the surprised exclamation that came from Cst. Smith. "Don't touch anything. I'll phone Chief Petrovic right now. Please stay at the Graysons' until we get in touch with you."

Cst. Smith hung up and for a moment I just stared at the phone.

FORTUNATELY, THE CHIEF was at home. Bob Petrovic was sitting in the front room, reading Saturday's paper and listening to his daughters argue. It was getting close to suppertime and the smell of roast beef was almost overwhelming. It was a scene of domestic bliss. When the phone rang, both girls knew it was for them. His oldest daughter grabbed the phone first. With a severe look of disappointment, she handed the phone to her dad.

"Constable Smith," she said in an accusatory tone.

Chief Petrovic reluctantly took the phone from his daughter. He knew it wouldn't be good news. A call to his home on Sunday evening from Cst. Smith *had* to be bad news.

"Petrovic here," he said with resignation. "Tell me all about it."

Cst. Smith started relating the story he'd just heard.

The chief interrupted him. "Did you say arm?"

Cst. Smith replied in the affirmative.

When Cst. Smith was finished, Chief Petrovic said: "Stay at the police station for the rest of your shift. I'll phone the Graysons."

The chief found their number and made the call. He thought he recognized the voice that answered.

"Is that Joel Franklin?" he said. "I thought you were back in town. I've seen you at the grocery store a few times. Cst. Smith just told me an incredible story. What happened today?"

Chief Petrovic listened as Joel told him about the arm and where it was found.

"Did you see any other body parts?" asked the chief.

"No sir," said Joel. "The area doesn't look like the scene of a crime."

"We can't do much today," said Chief Petrovic. "It's just about dark now. Sunset today is around 4:40 PM. I'll send Cst. Herman out as soon as I can locate him. He can mark the location and bring the severed arm to the station. We'll conduct a more thorough search tomorrow. Joel, can you please stay there to show Cst. Herman exactly where you found the arm?"

"Not a problem," said Joel. He sounded shaken.

Chief Petrovic ended the conversation.

CST. HERMAN KNOCKED on the Grayson's door about half an hour later. Supper was just about ready, but they had decided they would hold off sitting down to eat until they were finished with the police.

Jay Jarvis answered the door, then Jay and Joel escorted Cst. Herman out to the field where the arm lay. Cst. Herman planted a small yellow flag to mark the location of the discovery. He put the severed arm in a carrying bag, thanked them for promptly reporting what they had found, then headed back to the police station.

Monday, December 12th

JEREMIAH GRAYSON, SYLVIA'S dad, was not pleased when he looked out his window at lunchtime on Monday. There were quite a few cars parked along the street and along the edge of his front lawn. There were Model A and Model T Fords, two Chevrolets, a Dodge, and a couple of other vehicles. Parked nearby were a couple of buggies and a wagon pulled by a good-looking pair of Clydesdales. There were also some bicycles leaning against trees. The first vehicle to arrive had been the chief and a couple of his constables in their Ford Radio Motor Patrol Car. One of the constables had been busy making sure the parking was not chaotic. The chief was mustering the searchers and assigning areas for them to search.

To be fair, the chief of police had phoned Jeremiah early that morning and told him what to expect. Jeremiah and Clara Grayson were just surprised at the scope of the spectacle. Baby Brad was pretty excited at all the commotion. He appeared to like it.

EARLIER THAT MORNING, at 8:30, just as the sun was making its appearance, Chief Petrovic had had a brief meeting with his two constables.

With the end of temperance, and the onset of the depression, things had become more difficult to manage in Chaseford. Chief Petrovic needed more than two constables to help him keep things under control. Finances were tight, though, and while the chief knew Mayor

Thompson supported him, and Chief Petrovic had attended many council meetings to report on the increase in crime in town, he had not been permitted to add an additional constable.

At this morning's meeting, Chief Petrovic had instructed his constables to visit some of the businesses and talk to anyone they saw on the street about helping in a search. The constables were not to release any information at this time about what they were searching for. They were just to tell the people that they were needed for a search and where to meet. Interested parties were to dress warmly and be at the meeting place at noon.

On his way out to the Graysons', Chief Petrovic visited the local newspaper to explain the situation. He said the paper could put out a story about the search and make a request for anyone to come forward that had relevant information. The chief did not want to cause a panic but knew if there was no official story there definitely would be a panic as rumours spread from the people involved in the search. Sometimes you can't win. You just do your best.

The search was to take place in the fields behind the Grayson home. The land was owned by Dougal Van Bergen, an older man that owned quite a bit of land on the edge of town. Van Bergen told Chief Petrovic he could do what he wanted on that land because nothing else was happening on that land until spring.

Jeremiah Grayson had reluctantly agreed to allow the chief to use a small empty barn about forty feet from the north side of the Grayson home as a temporary headquarters for the search. The searchers were placed in groups of ten for instruction by the chief of police and given a specific area of land to search. If the searchers found anything suspicious they were told not to touch it. Instead, one of the constables was to be contacted so the item could be examined and the spot marked if necessary. Clara and some of the women from the Lutheran Church had agreed to provide hot drinks and sandwiches at 1:30 PM. Today's search would end at 5 o'clock. It would be close to dark by then. So the massive search started.

Word of the search spread fast even though the local paper wasn't out yet. Somehow, word got out that an arm had been found in the field. Now everyone was convinced that this was a search for body parts. People started contacting their relatives or friends to make sure they were not the missing body. This caused a bit of a panic among those who did think someone was missing.

At 5 o'clock the chief of police fired his shotgun into the air twice as a signal for the searchers to stop and to return to the temporary search headquarters at the barn. Once they arrived at the barn, they found the woodstove in full operation and hot coffee to drink. The searchers were glad for both. It had been cold out today. By 5:45, all the searchers had reported in, had their coffee, and left for home.

The chief of police appreciated all the help from the searchers, the Graysons, and the Ladies' Auxiliary of the local Lutheran Church. But despite everyone's efforts the search turned up nothing of significance. The chief of police was disappointed but not totally surprised. He still didn't know anything about the arm, but he hoped Dr. Whittles, the coroner, would be of some help.

I HADN'T TAKEN PART in the search. My mother wasn't feeling well, so I helped dad in the store instead. After supper at home at 200 Durham Street we sat around the table and talked. Mom was feeling somewhat better by mealtime so she was at the table too. I think today she had one of her migraines. A bad migraine can keep her in bed for two or three days. We did lots of speculating about the arm and about the missing body. From the next-door neighbour's son, who had taken part in the search, we knew that no other body parts had been found. Granny's reaction was a combination of disgust and curiosity. I think curiosity was winning out.

I said my goodbyes at about 7:30 and headed back to my apartment. These days, my accommodation was at my parents' store, Franklin's Groceries. It was only about a 15-minute walk from 200 Durham Street to the store. My apartment consisted of one makeshift room. I had my cot and lamp in a corner of the storeroom at the back of the store. My privacy wall was composed of stacks of canned goods boxes. There were variations in the height and length of my privacy wall depending on when we received our shipments. There was also a closet-sized bathroom with a toilet and a sink. The entrance to my quarters was a door at the back of the building beside the loading dock. My room wasn't overly warm, but that was okay. Thanks to Granny, mom, and Georgie, I had knitted sweaters, jackets, and socks.

The heat to the store, and to my luxury apartment, was provided by a coal furnace, which lived in a partial basement under the store. This octopus had more room than I did, but he needed it with all those big arms going all over the place. He was always hungry. One of my jobs was to feed the octopus. I had become quite used to shoveling coal.

Jay and I had talked briefly earlier in the day. He'd said he had an idea that he wanted to run by me. I invited him to drop over about 8 o'clock. When he arrived, we chatted for a bit. Jay had taken part in the search, so he was able to fill me in on all the details.

He stopped, looked at me, and said: "Here's my proposal. I think you and I should go and visit Chief Petrovic sometime tomorrow. I think we should offer our services as volunteer policemen."

"That's a great idea," I said.

It suddenly struck me that I was quite interested in police work. I had been at a loss as to what I was going to do with myself. I had my degree in business from Western, and that was good, but I didn't have a job or any prospects of one where the degree would be useful. I was back home again, helping out in the store. I felt like I'd gone from being 18 years old, to 21 years old, and back to 18 again. Maybe this would lead to an opportunity. I really liked the idea, in any case. We agreed to meet at the police station at 10 tomorrow morning.

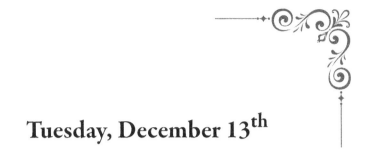

Tuesday, December 13th

CHIEF PETROVIC OPENED the door to his office Tuesday morning and welcomed us in.

"What can I do for you young men today?" he asked.

"Joel and I have talked this over," said Jay without preamble, "and we would like to volunteer our services to you on a regular basis. We understand you can't pay us, but we're interested in pursuing careers in policing, and serving in a voluntary capacity would enable us to gain valuable experience and help our community at the same time. You probably know I'm currently unemployed and that, since returning home from university, Joel is helping his dad at the grocery store."

The chief looked from one of us to the other and said: "You've caught me off guard. What does your dad think about this Joel? Will he have enough help?"

"I talked to my dad first thing this morning," I said. "He approved of the volunteering, provided I help him when I can."

"I'll have to talk to the mayor," said Chief Petrovic.

DR. FRANK WHITTLES, the coroner, met with Chief Petrovic at the hospital at 2 o'clock.

"Chief, this is a tricky one," said Dr. Whittles. "It appears to me that the arm was cut from the body using something heavy and blunt, probably an axe. This happened quite some time ago, but I don't know how long ago that was. There look to be something like teeth marks on several locations on the arm, but these marks are probably quite recent. I don't think they were caused by human teeth. They appear to be from a dog or wolf or similar animal."

"Do we need to involve the forensic people from Toronto again?" asked the chief. "You remember how helpful they were when we investigated the murder of Louise Carter back in 1928."

"Yes," replied Dr. Whittles. "I write back and forth on a fairly regular basis with Dr. Whitehead, who is still thoroughly engaged with his study of forensics. Dr. Whitehead is working out of a new laboratory in Toronto, established by the Attorney General of Ontario just a few months ago. Dr. Whitehead tells me his laboratory has up-to-date equipment, and forensic personnel in the laboratory are in regular contact with other forensic laboratories across North America. He's very excited about being there. I'll give him a call later today and see if we can make arrangements to send him the arm."

"Thanks, Frank," said Chief Petrovic. "The more information we can get, the more likely we are to solve this mystery."

After leaving Dr. Whittles at the hospital, the chief of police went to the mayor's office. Mayor Thompson had been elected for the first time in 1927. He was good at his job. He liked people and he liked to get things done. He was an honest man and would always give his opinion in a polite way. So when Chief Petrovic approached the mayor about having Jay Jarvis and Joel Franklin as volunteer policemen he knew he would get the mayor's answer directly. It would, of course, also require the approval of Town Council. But if the mayor approved, the council usually agreed. So the chief posed the question.

"I think it's an excellent idea," said Mayor Thompson. "As I recall, those two young fellows have already received medallions from the town for their contributions in the Louise Carter murder investigation. I know you're shorthanded, and I know you've just become involved in what is likely to be a difficult investigation with the appearance of that 'arm'. The council and I have talked about hiring more policemen – it will be necessary if we're going to have a sufficient police presence in town – and we've already decided to approve the hiring of an additional constable.

"Since these two young men have volunteered, I'm going to recommend we hire both of them. I'll put the names of those two fellows forward at the next council meeting on Monday night. They'll have to split the salary we were going to pay our one new constable. We can only afford to pay them $10 a week each. But from what you told me that's more than they expect. This could work out well for everyone. Until the approval, which could happen as soon as Monday evening, I leave it up to your discretion as to whether you use them on a voluntary basis. If you decide to use them now I will support your decision."

Chief Petrovic was thrilled. He thanked Mayor Thompson and informed him that he planned to contact both Jay and Joel that very day. The chief told him that, at this point in time, he would only tell them that they had been approved to be used on a voluntary basis.

Chief Petrovic returned to his office in a better mood than he had been in months. Being short two policemen had meant that, from time to time, he had to take shortcuts in some of the regular police duties. There were many situations that had arisen where he had only sent one constable when good practice would have been to send two. He and the town had been fortunate that nothing serious had happened to a policeman on those occasions. Chief Petrovic thought that, because it was a small town, where everyone knew their neighbour, they had been able to escape serious trouble when someone decided to act up. Now he could send two policemen and relax a bit. He phoned Jay Jarvis at the Grayson home and informed him that he was now a volunteer policeman. He could tell Jay was really pleased. The chief then dropped into Franklin's Groceries to deliver the news to Joel in person. The chief was pleased with Arthur Franklin's reaction. Arthur thanked the chief and congratulated his son.

Next, the chief of police got in touch with his two existing constables and told them they needed to meet with him at 4:30 in his office. Once they arrived and had a hot drink in front of them, Chief Petrovic told them the events of the day.

"You know we've been shorthanded for a while," began the chief. "You guys have worked hard and have done a good job. I now have some help for you. We're adding two volunteers to the force. Don't say anything to anyone yet because their appointments are not official until after the council meeting on Monday night. They don't have any police experience, but I have confidence in them."

"Who are they," asked Cst. Smith.

"Joel Franklin and Jay Jarvis are going to be helping us out," replied the chief. Both the young constables smiled.

"They're both good guys and we need all the help we can get," Cst. Herman said.

"It's going to work like this," said the chief. "I'm going to pair Joel up with you Cst. Herman, and I'm going to have Jay work with Cst. Smith." Both constables nodded in agreement. "Remember, they're new guys and you're going to have to help train them. Teach them the right things. If these pairings don't work out, let me know and we will change things." The chief could tell the two constables were so pleased that they almost wanted to dance a jig in front of him. He ended the meeting with: "Finish your shift. See you later."

CHIEF PETROVIC NEVER knew when he was going to get a phone call at home. What he did know was that when he did get one at home in the evening it was always significant. When his youngest daughter handed him the phone he heard a breathless voice say:

"This is Ginny Fairfield. We live on the eighth concession about a mile or so out of town."

When she paused, Chief Petrovic thought: *She's trying not to cry.*

Ginny continued in a wavering voice. "I'm alone out here with the kids right now. Colin isn't back till tomorrow. When I opened the back door, the dog brought in what looks like a man's leg." She started to sob.

Chief Petrovic did his best to calm her down. When she quieted, he said: "I think you live right next to the Harbinger farm?"

"Yes," said Ginny. "Please, I need help now."

"I'll have a policeman out to see you as soon as possible," said the chief. "Make sure your outside lights are on."

Chief Petrovic phoned Cst. Herman.

"Get in touch with your new sidekick, Joel Franklin," he said. "The two of you need to go out to the Fairfield Place on the eighth concession. It's next to the Harbinger farm. The family dog just brought a man's leg home."

There was a pause at the other end of the line. "A man's leg? A real man's leg?" Cst. Herman stuttered.

"According to Ginny Fairfield, yes. I suspect it's from the same body as the arm that we found on Sunday. Get out to the Fairfield Place as soon as you can."

CST. HERMAN AND VOLUNTEER constable Joel Franklin found the Fairfield farm without a problem. They were both still kind of stunned by this latest development. Cst. Herman knocked on the side door and a little wide-eyed boy opened it.

"Come on in," he said. "My mom's here in the kitchen. She doesn't feel too good."

The two policemen came through the side door into the kitchen and found Ginny sitting at the table, looking very pale. There were three little boys in the kitchen with her, from 5 to 8 years of age. Joel couldn't tell whether they were terrified or supremely excited. There was a dog barking and growling in the room behind the kitchen. That door was shut tight.

"Blackie's really mad," said the oldest little boy. "Ma took the leg away from him. I felt it. It's too hard for Blackie to eat anyway."

"Where's the leg now?" asked Cst. Herman.

"It's in the wood box over here," said the next oldest boy.

Cst. Herman had Joel put the leg in the sack they'd brought with them for that purpose, then the two of them stayed and talked with Ginny Fairfield for a few minutes. They thanked her for getting in touch with the chief then they left. Chief Petrovic told them to deliver the leg to the hospital. Dr. Whittles would deal with it tomorrow.

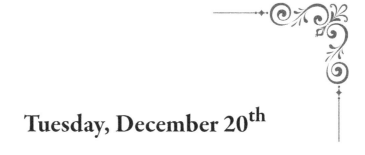

Tuesday, December 20th

ALL FIVE POLICEMEN, including the two volunteers, were in Chief Petrovic's office at 9 o'clock Tuesday morning. They all knew that, counting Tuesday's discovery at Colin and Ginny Fairfield's farm, they had now forwarded two arms, two legs, and a head to Dr. White-head's forensic lab in Toronto. The last three gruesome discoveries had just been sent yesterday afternoon. The policemen cautiously looked at each other around the table.

"We're all thinking the same thing," said Chief Petrovic. "I hope we don't find any more body parts."

Everyone sighed and nodded in agreement.

On this past Saturday afternoon, a group of hunters in the bush north of town found an arm. On Sunday morning, as parishioners were coming out of the United Church on the edge of Sedgwick, a small village north of Chaseford, one of the local dogs was seen dragging a leg down the street. Two teenage boys collared the dog, and, with strenuous efforts, took the leg away from it. Later that same day, a totally bald head was found in the ditch on the tenth concession about 2 miles from town.

The town hadn't panicked yet but there was a certain undercurrent of fear. No one – man or woman – was going out at night alone; especially in the country. The newspaper was doing its best to inform people and to keep them calm, but as more body parts appeared, it became more and more difficult. Children were being escorted to and from school and older people who lived alone were being checked on every day by friends and family. Adding to the mystery was that no one was apparently missing.

The constables sat at the table and waited for Chief Petrovic to lay out his plan.

"I'm going to start with the good news," he said.

"What's the good news?" asked Cst. Smith.

"When I reached the office this morning, just after 8 o'clock, the mayor dropped in and handed this letter to me," said Chief Petrovic. "It reads as follows:

> *Dear Chief Petrovic,*
>
> *It gives me great pleasure to announce to you that at last night's in camera council meeting the council unanimously agreed to provide you with two more police constables. Cst. Jay Jarvis and Cst. Joel Franklin are hereby appointed to your staff. Their status as constables has been dated from the start of the day this past Monday, December 19th. They will each receive a salary of $10 a week.*
>
> *Enclosed please find two letters. One letter for Jay and another for Joel congratulating them on their appointments.*
>
> *Sincerely,*
>
> *Alvin Thompson, mayor of Chaseford."*

Constables Smith and Herman cheered while the new constables Franklin and Jarvis beamed ecstatically. After a few happy moments of congratulations, the chief said:

"Let's do some thinking."

Chief Petrovic went to the cupboard and pulled out a large, rolled-up map. A map holder bracket had been installed a couple of years ago on the wall behind his desk and he hung the map on the bracket. When the chief pulled the map down, everyone could see that it was a map of Chaseford and the surrounding area. It was not a full county map. The chief took some thumbtacks and placed them in the locations where the body parts had been found.

"Do any of you see any pattern in the way the body parts we've found are distributed?" asked the chief.

"It might be difficult to determine a pattern, since it seems that these parts have been dragged from their original positions at least once – and maybe more than once – by curious and hungry dogs or other animals," said Cst. Herman.

"Any other comments?" asked the chief.

New constable Jarvis said: "I have a couple of ideas."

Everyone turned and looked at him.

"Keep talking," said the chief.

"If you figured out approximately where the centre of the circle was that encompassed these five sightings, and then drew a circle that was somewhat larger so that it included the five sightings and some of the land beyond, that might give you an area where we should look for more clues," said Jay. "If we're lucky, maybe we can find the source of all these body parts."

"That sounds like a good idea," said Cst. Smith, "but it sounds pretty mathematical to me."

"You mentioned another idea, Cst. Jarvis," said the chief.

"Yes," said Jay. "This may be iffy, but everything's happened to the north of town. So instead of a circle you could use a band of land that included the sightings and then just extend that band in the same direction to the north five or six miles. At least to start with. That would give you another area to focus on."

Chief Petrovic looked around the table and realized he wasn't the only one that wasn't entirely certain what Cst. Jarvis was saying.

"You're going to have to make this easier for us to visualize," the chief said. "Our secretary Sherry Simpson can help you get some supplies. Then you can prepare maps for us that show the sighting location and the two areas you described. Can you have those maps or diagrams ready for a meeting at 9 o'clock Friday morning?"

"Yes sir," answered Cst. Jarvis with enthusiasm. He was clearly glad to be able to contribute.

AT 2 O'CLOCK THAT AFTERNOON, Dr. Whittles appeared at the door to the chief of police's office. He rapped on the door and heard Chief Petrovic say: "Come on in."

When the chief saw who it was, he said: "You must have some news to report. I take it Dr. Whitehead has been in touch with you with some forensic information."

"He has," answered Dr. Whittles. "What he's told me so far won't make your job any easier."

"Just tell me what he found out," said the chief.

"Understand that they haven't completed their examination of the last three body parts we sent to them on Monday," said Dr. Whittles. "This information only applies to the first arm and leg we forwarded. Take a look at Dr. Whitehead's letter yourself."

Chief Petrovic read the following extract from the letter:

1. The arm and the leg are from two different bodies. At this point in our forensic investigation, it appears that the arm is from a male and the leg is from a female. Both limbs appear to be from adult bodies.

2. The body parts appear to have been frozen for a long time, implying they have not been recently severed from a torso.

3. We have no way to determine how long ago the bodies were frozen. We cannot give an accurate timeline.

"Hmm," said the chief. "This certainly is not the report I anticipated. Strange as it seems, after reading this, I think we should be looking for a location where bodies could be stored and frozen."

Dr Whittles just stared at him.

WHEN I SHOWED UP AT my parents' house a little after 6 o'clock everyone hollered 'Congratulations!'

There was a big celebration at the Franklin home that evening. Granny Watson had spent most of the day in the kitchen, baking two apple pies and getting a roast beef ready for supper. As soon as Emmylou came in from school, Granny put her to work too. Emmylou was 12 and in grade 7 at Chaseford Public School. She could be very helpful when motivated. My mom pitched in too, as soon as she got back from the store. They wanted to surprise me with a party celebrating my new position as a police constable.

Now I'm contributing too, I thought, delighted.

When our visit and supper was over I excused myself. I had to get some sleep now that I was a defender of the public, I said. They laughed and I headed for the door. On my way out, Granny handed me what was left of the pie.

"I know you'll need a snack," she said.

With a full stomach and a pie in my hand, I headed home to the store.

As soon as I entered the store through the back door, Walter said (or sent): "Glad you had a good time tonight. You deserve it."

Walter still resided at 200 Durham Street, as he always would, and we had talked every night since I had come back to Chaseford. When I was in London at University, we didn't communicate directly the way we could now. I would check with him once a week, but it was usually through an intermediary essence. These messages kept me well informed about what was going on at 200 Durham Street. Our skills had improved, but our long-range communication still wasn't good for much more than a couple of miles. Some essences had far greater sensitivities and corresponding ranges than me and Walter, but the store was well within our communication range.

Walter and I discussed the 'body parts investigation'. He told me that he had been in touch with local essences but that none of them were aware of any situations where bodies had been dismembered. Walter and I agreed that anyone faced with the prospect of dismemberment would be in an extreme state of anxiety and anger. It was this type of situation that resulted in people like Walter and Louise Carter remaining as electromagnetic presences, or *essences*, as Walter and I had decided to call them. Walter said that he would continue to check around and that if he found anyone with information he would tell me where to find them.

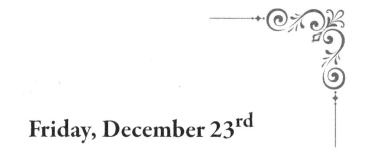

Friday, December 23rd

IT WAS 9 O'CLOCK FRIDAY morning. Chief Petrovic started the meeting by reminding everyone of the potluck supper at his place that night at six.

"Our first item of business today," he then said, "is an examination of the maps that Cst. Jarvis has prepared."

Jay had made copies of the maps for everyone on 18-inch-wide shelving paper. It was a good size to work with for this project. He handed out the maps and briefly explained what they showed. You could tell he had spent a lot of time on the drawings.

Cst. Herman complemented Jay on the maps and then turned to the chief. "Is the plan to visit all the properties shown in the two areas outlined on the map?"

"It's the best plan we have for now," replied the chief. "Unless someone comes forward with information about the body parts, we're just going to have to use good old-fashioned police work and do a lot of walking and talking. This could be a long investigation." The chief added: "The time that Jay has spent on preparing these maps is much appreciated.

"Another arm was discovered yesterday," he continued. "It was found well within the area Jay has shown on his maps. That makes me feel that Jay's maps are a good starting point.

"I also have some news from the forensic lab in Toronto. I was really concerned after reading the latest letter from Dr. Whitehead. What bothered me the most, aside from the horrific nature of the crime, was the second point in Dr. Whitehead's summary, which was as follows: 'The body parts appear to have been frozen for a long time'. Implying they have not been recently severed from a torso."

"I think I understand what you're suggesting, Chief," I said. "The fact that the crime could have occurred any time over a large number of years makes finding the crime site extremely difficult."

"Thank you, Joel. You're correct. In fact, the crime scene may no longer exist," said the chief.

"So are we trying to do something that's impossible?" asked Cst. Smith.

They all looked at one another.

"Not impossible, but extremely difficult," the chief answered.

"Earlier in the meeting, Chief, you said we would have to do a lot of walking and talking," said Cst. Herman. "From what you've just said now, it seems to me that we have to look at all current buildings on all the properties and also look at all the building sites of buildings that may have been torn down in the past. I'm not certain how we're going to locate the sites of buildings that are no longer standing. In other words, we have to look everywhere, and when we look, we have to take to notice of whether the configuration of the land has changed at all in the last fifty years. Sir, that sounds to me like a huge chore."

"It is a huge chore, Cst. Herman," said the chief. "I want all of you to get a lot of rest over Christmas because we will be doing a lot of walking and talking after that. Does anyone have any other ideas?"

"Jay does excellent work," said Cst. Smith. "I'm wondering about another map or an addition to this map. I think if a body part was found by a dog, and if we know where the dog's home is, we should show that home as a point on the map as well."

"Good idea," said Chief Petrovic. "Let's incorporate those lines on the map, too, Jay."

IT WAS THE LAST FRIDAY before Christmas. Chief Petrovic and his wife had decided they would host a potluck supper at 6 o'clock for all four constables and our wives or girlfriends and children. Aside from the chief's two teenage daughters, there would be six children present. That meant Chief Petrovic would have to wear his Santa suit.

I was the only constable not married, but my fiancée Georgie was attending the party with me. Cst. Herman and his wife had a little boy of seven and a little girl of four. Cst. Smith had two boys, four years old and six years old. Jay and Sylvia were bringing Baby Brad. Brad was fifteen months old and he had mastered walking. He had reached a dangerous age because he could crawl fast and pull himself up to his feet. He was a very curious boy.

The chief's two teenage girls had been told ahead of time they were on babysitting duty. They looked forward to this, especially to helping with Baby Brad. The chief and his wife were supplying the turkey and the Christmas pudding. Everyone else had a list of food to bring.

It turned out to be a great evening. The food was good and there was plenty of it. There was lots of squealing from little voices and a constant babble of adult voices. Just after the table had been cleared, and everyone was comfortably seated, Cst. Herman's little boy suddenly said: "I hear bells."

"Let's be quiet and listen," said Chief Petrovic's oldest girl.

Everyone hushed.

"I hear the bells now," said Cst. Herman's daughter.

"I think the sound of bells is coming from outside the front door," said Georgie. "Maybe one of you should go open it?"

The little boy who had first heard the bells ran and opened the front door. He was so startled that he jumped back. Santa was there with a bag full of toys.

Santa Ho-Ho-Ho'd his way into the living room and sat in Chief Petrovic's favourite chair. The gift-giving and fooling went on for an hour.

Everyone got a gift except Chief Petrovic. He must've been called away on police business. Santa left after he'd had a hot drink of cider and a piece of Christmas cake. Shortly after, the chief returned and asked the small children if anything exciting had happened while he was gone. That resulted in another ten minutes of happy babbling as small voices explained the visit that had occurred.

At the end of the evening, just as everybody was retrieving their winter gear and getting ready to head home, Chief Petrovic's youngest daughter came and whispered something to him.

"Keep the dog in the back room," said the chief. "Once everyone has left, I'll go out and take a look."

After all the goodbyes Chief Petrovic went to the back, closed-in porch to see the dog and the human arm he had brought home with him.

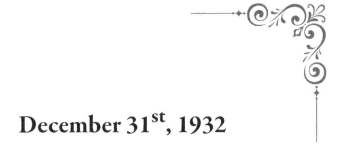

December 31st, 1932

1932 HAD BEEN A DIFFICULT year for everyone I knew, and probably for most other people in the world. The Great Depression just seemed to keep going and going. For Jay and me, though, things had brightened up a bit. We had paying jobs. The pay was very low at $10 a week, but we felt good because we were doing something we enjoyed.

I invited Georgie to my place for New Year's Eve. Jay and Sylvia were coming too. Georgie came over early. She brought a few balloons she had purchased as well as some coloured paper chains she had made. Georgie said we were going to make my small space into an enchanted party room for our New Year's celebration.

When she came in, smiling as usual, I couldn't resist. I kissed her and asked her to marry me. She looked at me and said, "I love you, Joel, but I thought we'd decided we needed more time to be financially ready?"

I answered by taking an engagement ring out of my jacket pocket.

"I have a job now," I said, "and when I see the happiness that Jay and Sylvia have, I want to start sharing my life with you now."

Georgie kissed me again. "Let's get married," she said. Then she added: "Is this is a real ring?"

We both laughed and kissed again.

Jay and Sylvia arrived at about 8 o'clock. Sylvia's parents, the Graysons, were having another couple in to help them welcome the New Year, so Sylvia's mom was glad to look after Baby Brad. Clara was a proud grandma and probably couldn't wait to show off her first grandson. We had snacks and drinks for the evening and a bottle of good wine that Cst. Smith had given me that I had saved for the occasion. Jay was a bit of a history buff and I knew from previous New Year's Eves he would want to talk about big events from the past year.

By 9 o'clock, after our first glass of wine, Jay said – trying to sound like the voice in the *Movietone News* – "It's time for the year in review." Then, in a more normal voice: "I want everyone to tell me what they thought was the biggest story from 1932."

"That's easy for me," said Sylvia, "but it is a terrible story. It was the kidnapping and murder of the Lindbergh baby back in March. He was only a few months older than Brad Junior. If that happened to Brad Junior, I don't know whether I'd want to live."

"They haven't caught the kidnappers yet," said Jay, "but it's such a high-profile case that I know they'll catch them."

"I'm scared to death of what's happening in Germany," I said. "I think the Nazis will eventually take over. After the election in July, the Nazis had gained far more seats than any other party since the last election. With the unemployment rate jumping from 8.5% to 30% in Germany because of the depression, the German people want a strong personality to lead them. I'm convinced that if Hitler has the opportunity, he'll declare himself a leader responsible to no one. A dictatorship in a powerful country by a man like Hitler spells an awful lot of trouble for the rest of the world."

"You're painting a scary picture, Joel," said Georgie. "My biggest story of this year is the surprise engagement between me and Joel." Then she flashed her ring. It didn't flash much.

Immediately, Jay's year-in-review ended. Sylvia and Georgie were hugging and babbling. Jay shook my hand.

"How did you ever get her to agree to marry you?" he said. "You're a lucky man."

After that announcement, we opened the bottle of wine early. We finished the wine with toasts as midnight rolled by into 1933.

After Jay and Sylvia left, Georgie and I sat at the small card table I had set up in my room. I looked at her and said, "I love you, and I really want to marry you, but I have to tell you something first."

"Aha," she said. "True confessions. You're supposed to tell me these things before you propose."

"I know," I said, "but you looked so beautiful tonight that I got carried away. You know I love you."

"Confess," she said.

I told her the story of Walter. I even showed her the scar from the lightning. I told her that something in my brain had been stimulated by the lightning, and that this stimulation had resulted in my ability to communicate with Walter. I told her that I communicated with Walter regularly. I told her I could talk to him or communicate to him right now if I wanted to. I told her how important he had been in helping me find the medallion that led to the successful conclusion of the Louise Carter murder investigation. I told her he wasn't present anywhere except 200 Durham Street. At that address, he wasn't detectable to anyone but me or someone else if they had the special ability I had. I told her she wouldn't see him or notice him. I told her he posed no danger to anyone. He couldn't cause harm because he couldn't physically do anything. I told her that Walter and I had agreed to use the term essence to describe him. I told her no one else knew my secret, not even my parents or Jay.

When I finished, Georgie had lots of questions. Her first question was, "Are you crazy?"

"I don't think so," I answered. "But I am different."

"You certainly are," she replied.

We both laughed.

"I'll kiss you one more time to see if you still seem the same," she said.

We kissed again, and she said, "You're still the same."

After talking some more, Georgie seemed satisfied that I wasn't insane and we talked about the wedding. We decided to get married on Saturday, June 3rd.

"It's after 1 o'clock," said Georgie. "You better walk me home so I can break the news of our engagement to my parents. Your other secret is safe with me."

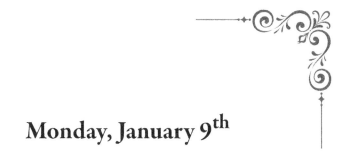

Monday, January 9th

THE CHRISTMAS AND NEW Year's season had been hectic for everyone. Jay and Joel got their first taste of domestic disputes and breaking up fights and other public disturbances owing to excessive alcohol consumption. This time of year brought out either the best or the worst in everyone. Not everyone was hearing the message of peace on earth and goodwill to all. The rookie constables weathered it, though, and soon learned that they would end up taking the odd punch in the course of duty.

At 9 o'clock Monday morning, everyone met in Chief Petrovic's office. He looked around at them and said, "Aside from the odd bruise, you guys look pretty good."

"They're learning sir," said Cst. Herman.

"They're getting better at ducking at the right time," said Cst. Smith.

The three experienced policemen chuckled. The most the rookies could muster was a smile.

"I have some exciting news for you," said the chief. "We're going to embark on a long journey."

"I believe you meant to say: 'a long, paid-for, relaxing journey to a warmer climate,'" said Cst. Smith.

"Not exactly," the chief replied. "I shouldn't have used the word 'we' in connection with the journey. The correct word is 'you.'"

"It sounds like you have a big exhausting job for us," said Cst. Herman.

The chief of police got up and retrieved the five copies of the map that Jay had produced in December. He handed them around the table. Then he said, "We have all admired Jay's mapwork. Now we're going to use it. As I told you back in December, this will not be easy work. It will require a lot of walking and talking. If we're going to uncover any clues that will lead us to the solution of this 'body parts mystery' we will have to investigate, for a start, every one of the properties shown on this map."

"Sir, I believe there are over a hundred properties on the map," said Cst. Herman.

"There are over a hundred and ten properties to be searched thoroughly, Cst. Herman," said the chief. "This is a daunting task. The four of you will set up a schedule to ensure that only one pair of you are out searching at a time. I need one pair of constables in town for regular duty and for any emergencies that may occur. We don't have much daylight this time of year, so schedule accordingly. We will only conduct the searches when we can see. That means on bad weather days we will not be out searching. When that happens, you do not miss a turn; instead, you take the next available good weather day. If someone is ill or absent for some other reason, then I expect the four of you to work out an equitable solution.

"You're to carry on for the rest of the morning with your normal duties. I want the four of you to sit down at 1:30 this afternoon to prepare the search schedule. I want the first search team to start tomorrow. At the end of every search day you're to report back to me at the office before 5 o'clock.

"When you report in, you are to tell me what property you searched and what the result was. I'm going to post my copy of Jay's map on the wall behind my desk. When the search of a property is completed I will put a note on that property on the map with the date and the search team responsible. This will be more fun than you ever wanted over the next few months."

They didn't know whether to grin or grimace. A grimace seemed most appropriate.

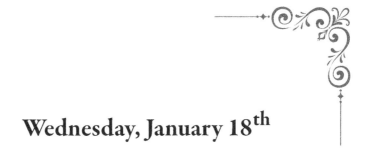

Wednesday, January 18th

CONSTABLE PETER HERMAN and I were going out on search duty for our third time. Jay and Cst. Smith, the other search team, had been out to search farms twice. We haven't been able to go out every day. The weather has been cold and there has been a lot of snow. We had quite a storm the past weekend. Someone who'd come into the grocery store had told my dad that they'd measured a depth of 37 inches of snow in a sheltered area. The drifts were much higher of course. Most of the snow fell last Sunday and Monday.

Everyone loves a sleigh ride, but when it's 19 degrees below zero Fahrenheit and the wind is howling no one wants to go out. Since the weekend storm, this is the first day we dared to go out on a search.

Searching these farms is more difficult than I had anticipated. This time of year, you can't easily walk the land and you can't necessarily see very far. But we have had lots of practice snowshoeing. So far, we've limited our actual search time on a property to about three hours. By the time we get our things together and prepare for the search, travel to our destination, perform the search, and get back to the police station, the total time it takes us is usually well over four hours.

Today, Cst. Herman and I are headed to the Conrad farm. We make certain at least two days ahead of time that we have permission from the property owners to visit. We've had to reschedule a couple of times in order to accommodate people, but no one has refused us yet. I don't think anyone will. Between the newspaper articles and all the talk in town generated by the gruesome appearance of the body parts, everyone is hoping we will solve the mystery quickly. People are still very concerned about their personal safety, even though the paper has stressed that it appears the body parts we are finding, according to forensics experts from Toronto, are not from recent murders.

IT IS NECESSARY FOR the landowners to be cooperative because we are going to be looking through their home as well as any outbuildings. We also ask them to either mark the sites of any torn-down buildings on the property or to escort us to those sites. We examine the buildings and the sites first, before we start to walk the land.

The Conrad farm is a little over two miles out of town. It's a one hundred-acre farm. There is no bush on the farm, although there are a few trees. This farm has a one-and-a-half-story farmhouse, a timber frame barn, a small pig barn, and another shed. There are also the remains of another old house that used to be on the property.

We arrived at the property at about 1:30 in the afternoon. Mrs. Conrad and her two youngest children, who were not old enough to go to school, were in the house. She was in the kitchen with the kids doing some baking. Her husband Roger was in the barn. We went to the barn and talked to Roger for a few minutes. He wanted the latest update on how our investigation was going and whether we had found any more body parts. Then he went with us on our tour of the house, the barn, and the other outbuildings. Next, Roger took us to the site where the old house had stood. We poked through the site, but it was obvious that it was not the place we were looking for.

"I'm glad I don't have to do the searching you're doing," Roger said. "I know you have to do it, but it must seem like a waste of time. I don't think you're looking for a needle in a haystack; I think you're looking for a needle in the entire hay production of Canada last year."

We laughed at his joke.

"How do you go about conducting the search?" he asked. "You must have some kind of method or you could be walking all over the place and not be sure where you had looked and where you hadn't."

"Did you notice that coil rope I have over my shoulder?" I said. "It's about one chain in length, or 66 feet."

"Hold on," said Roger, "don't tell me any more. I think I figured it out. Most of the farms are about 20 chains wide. So, you take one end of the rope, and Cst. Herman takes the other end, and then you guys walk from one end of the farm to the other about 20 times."

"Congratulations," said Cst. Herman. "You were very clever to figure out our method that quickly. Maybe you'd like to accompany us while we do your farm?"

Roger smiled and said, "No, you guys are the experts. I'll leave the job to you."

"Sometimes it gets a little more complicated, like when we encounter ponds or trees or fences or other obstacles," said Cst. Herman, "but we certainly do get a lot of good exercise. As you know, these farms have a lot more depth than they have width. Our method isn't fancy, but we think we get the land pretty thoroughly covered."

"You guys have quite a task ahead of you," said Roger. "I think you need some refreshments before you head out to cover the land. Come on back to the kitchen for a hot cup of tea and a piece of cake."

We accepted enthusiastically, not wanting to offend him. About fifteen minutes later, we left the house. We told Roger we would start walking the land at the southeast corner of his property, near the road, and then follow the fence line to the back of his farm. We told him it usually took us more than one day to do a farm. We would come and knock at his door somewhere around 4:30 to let him know we were done for the day. We would then put a small yellow flag near the edge of the road at the end of our last back-and-forth trip. Then the next time we returned, the flag would be our starting point.

WE SET OUT.

We were almost to the back of the farm, on our fourth trip, when we noticed the sky had darkened. Within a couple of minutes, the wind had picked up and it had started to snow.

We were in the wrong place at the wrong time. The wind was blowing all the loose snow from last weekend's storm around and it was snowing heavily on top of that. It took us less than two minutes to realize we were in trouble. We couldn't see each other, and with the noise of the storm, we couldn't hear each other, either. We couldn't see *anything*. Fortunately, we each still held an end of the rope. Acting on instinct, we followed the rope until we met.

I was scared, and I think Peter was as scared as I was. We were not prepared for this kind of emergency. We didn't even have our guns with us. We'd left them back in the car.

"We don't know where we are, and we don't know how long we are going to be out here, so we'd better start to think about how we are going to survive," said Cst. Herman.

"I'm getting cold already out in this wind," I said. "We need some shelter."

"Do you remember – I think it was on our second trip to the end of the farm – not far from the back there was a small group of trees," said Cst. Herman. "We need to find that copse of trees." Then he added, "We can search more area if we each cover some ground, but it is very important that we don't get separated. Tie your end of the rope around you, and I'll tie my end around me. Even if we can't see each other, we will know where the other person is by tugging the rope. Three sharp tugs mean either we found the trees or there's a problem."

I let Cst. Herman get a few steps ahead of me and then we both headed back in what we thought was the direction of the trees.

We had been wandering around blindly like this for about fifteen minutes when I suddenly felt three pulls on the rope. I thought I heard a yell. It was hard to be sure I'd heard anything over the roar of the wind, because when the wind changed its speed, the pitch of its howl changed as well. If you had a good imagination, you would think it was talking to you. When I tried to move, I could tell the other end of the rope was fixed somewhere. That meant Cst. Herman was stuck. Had he fallen? Was he injured? Those were the first two questions that went through my mind.

I started to shorten the rope. I couldn't reel it in, because it was fixed at the other end, but I could pull myself toward that point. I followed the rope for a minute and then suddenly heard another yell. I was a lot closer to Cst. Herman now and I could make out the word '**help!**' That was definitely Peter, and he was nearby.

I came to a stop and then I moved ahead very slowly. I couldn't see a thing, but I heard Peter holler help again and realized he must only be a few feet away. I pulled on the rope and he pulled back. I knew he was trapped somehow, and I didn't want to end up the same way, so I crouched low to the ground and inched my way ahead. I thought I could hear a splashing noise.

I hollered at Cst. Herman and it seemed his reply came from about five feet away.

"Stop," he shouted. "You must be at the edge of the pond. Don't come any closer. Just pull me out."

We had forgotten about the pond. On our second trip from the front to the back of the farm we'd had to skirt the edge of a pond. It had been hard to see because of the all the snow, but Roger Conrad had told us about it. He'd said the milder patch of weather before the recent heavy snows had left the ice very thin in the middle of the pond. So we'd known it was there, but I think the blizzard had caused us to panic a bit. We'd remembered the group of trees but forgot about the pond.

I braced my feet and pulled on the rope. As Peter got closer to me I could hear his teeth chattering. I managed to get him out, but he was soaked to the waist. He hadn't hurt himself, he just hadn't been able to get himself out of the water. I knew we now had an even greater problem: Peter was too wet to survive long in this storm. If we didn't find some shelter very soon he would die.

The one good thing about Peter stumbling into the pond was that we had now also found the copse of trees we'd been looking for, and they might provide us with some shelter. Peter was shivering almost uncontrollably but he could still walk so we carefully made our way around the edge of the pond. Within two or three minutes we had found the clump of trees. Each of us had a small hatchet so we were able to hack off some branches and build a kind of lean-to shelter beside the largest tree. That helped, but it wasn't going to be enough to save Peter.

I don't smoke but I always carry matches in case of an emergency. It turned out to be a good idea. One of the trees was dead and had been for some time. It was not buried in the snow and was propped up against a couple of the other trees. I was able to get some kindling by breaking off some of the smaller branches and then breaking them into pieces. That gave us some wood that would be a little easier to ignite. I built a pile of kindling in the middle of our little shelter and then from my backpack I took out one of the matchbooks from Mabel's Diner. My matches were dry and within a couple of minutes we had a little fire going. Peter was sitting as close to the fire as he possibly could, but he was shivering and extremely uncomfortable. The storm was still raging pretty good. According to my watch it was about 6 o'clock; suppertime. I was really concerned. I didn't know how long Peter would last even with the fire that I was feeding.

Would the Conrads think we had left the farm earlier? They had no reason to worry about us. Because of our police duties, Cst. Herman and I didn't always get home at a specific time. We were usually home for supper but sometimes we were late. We hadn't checked into the office, but with the storm maybe the chief was busy doing other things? How long was it going to be before anyone noticed we were missing? If we were late, they wouldn't start worrying about us for a few hours at least. I thought that was going to be far too long. I thought I might be okay overnight, but I was pretty certain Peter couldn't last that long.

I CONCENTRATED AND contacted Walter. I knew Walter couldn't physically help me. But I had an idea.

"Walter can you hear me?"

"I can sense you, Joel."

I focused my concentration and sent as clear a message as I could, explaining the situation to Walter. I told him it was a matter of life or death. I told Walter where we were and that I had a plan.

After a pause, Walter sent back: "I understand the urgency. What is your plan?"

"In one of our early conversations in the attic, in the summer of 1928, you mentioned there was another person living in Chaseford, or nearby, that has the same ability that I possess," I communicated back. "I understood from you that it was a woman. I don't know who she is, but since I haven't heard of her, I assume that she wants to remain anonymous. I think we can save Cst. Herman, and preserve her secrecy, if we follow my plan. I know you can't contact the woman directly, but you can contact her essence and then her essence can contact her."

I paused to clear my head. The need to remain clearly focused on the information I was broadcasting made these lengthy communications very tiring. After a moment, I continued.

"For this plan to work, this other person has to contact my fiancée Georgie as soon as possible. Georgie knows about my talent and Georgie knows about you. This other person can contact Georgie, and – without revealing her name – inform Georgie that Cst. Herman and I are in a desperate situation at the back of the Conrad farm, near the pond, and that Cst. Herman requires medical attention. Georgie should then contact Chief Petrovic and explain that I was to phone her from the police station at 5 o'clock to make arrangements for dinner at

6 o'clock tonight. She can't find me, and my parents don't know where I am."

I had to pause again. I was getting tired and losing focus. There was no time to spare, so after a momentary rest I continued with the message.

"Georgie is to tell the chief she's contacted Peter Herman's wife and Peter's wife is worried about him. Peter always phones her if he's going to be late. Georgie is to tell the chief she is convinced that Peter and I are trapped somehow at the back of the Conrad farm. Georgie is to tell the chief she thinks we've encountered danger of some kind. She's to tell him that they need to search for us right away and that if they won't she'll get my dad to help her form a local search team. Georgie has to convince the chief there's no time to waste."

"That's a good plan, Joel," Walter sent back. "I think we'll get cooperation as long as this woman can remain anonymous. I'll get in touch with the other essence immediately."

Walter was gone. The wind began to die down. I kept feeding the fire and soon had to cut some more branches. Peter was still somewhat aware, but he told me he just wanted to sleep. He was mumbling, and I wondered if he wasn't a little confused. I checked my watch. It was now almost 7:30. It was relatively calm now, but it was very cold. It was clearing up and I could see some stars.

They have to get here soon, I thought. *I don't know how much longer Peter will last.*

I cut more wood, built up the fire, and checked my watch again. 8 o'clock. I contacted Walter.

"What happened?" I projected.

"So far as I know, that other woman contacted Georgie within half an hour of our conversation," Walter immediately replied.

"I don't know what else to do," I said. "I'm fine, but I'm really worried about Peter. He's asleep but I don't think that's a good sign."

"All you can do is be patient," was Walter's reply.

The communication with Walter was important to me. It was keeping me going. I didn't feel quite so alone and isolated with Walter around.

TEN MINUTES LATER I could hear voices.

I started to shout: "Over here! Over here! Over here!"

"We're on our way. We see your fire," I heard someone shout back.

Soon I could see lanterns and hear people talking excitedly to one another. I heard someone shout: "Watch out!" Someone else said: "That was close. Thanks for the warning."

I guess they found the pond.

A group of men was suddenly at our campsite: Chief Petrovic, constables Smith and Jay Jarvis, Roger Conrad, and my dad. I couldn't believe what I was seeing. They explained that it had been a very difficult walk to the back of the farm, even in snowshoes. Fortunately, the wind had died down and visibility wasn't too bad. The biggest problem now was the depth of the snow. They'd taken turns being in the lead; that way, the path was broken somewhat for those following. They'd brought a good-sized sleigh with them and had attached a six-foot long wooden platform, about three feet wide, to the back. The sleigh was loaded with blankets, shovels, and a basket packed with food and drinks.

Chief Petrovic took a look at Cst. Herman and said, "He's still breathing, but it seems to be shallow. I'm really concerned about his condition. We need to get those wet clothes off him and get him wrapped in these blankets. Then we need to get him on the sleigh and get him back to your house, Roger, as soon as possible. Hopefully, Dr. Fitzgerald will be at your home by the time we get there. I called him just before I left town and told him where your farm was. He said he'd been there once before, when your oldest boy fell out of the apple tree."

Cst. Herman was still asleep. He seemed unaware of the noise and the commotion. Even moving him to the pallet didn't wake him.

We were back in the farmhouse in less than thirty minutes. There were already several people at the house when we carried Peter into the kitchen from the side porch. Georgie rushed up and gave me a hug and whispered in my ear, "I'm glad you know Walter."

A small cot had been set up in the parlour. We laid Peter down on it and got out of the way so he could be tended to by Dr. Fitzgerald. After a brief examination, Dr. Fitzgerald turned to us and said: "His breathing could be stronger, but his pulse is steady. His body temperature is slightly less than 94°. That means he's suffering from hypothermia and he's in some danger if it doesn't go up, but I expect, because he's now indoors and in a warm location, his body temperature will increase back to normal. I don't see any signs of severe frostbite. I think he'll be fine. If possible, he shouldn't be moved until tomorrow."

Peter's wife, who had been in tears since we arrived, thanked Dr. Fitzgerald. Then she thanked the rest of us for rescuing Peter. Then she burst into tears again and sat down on the edge of the cot next to her husband.

From the kitchen, Mrs. Conrad announced: "The muffins I've been baking are ready. I also have a kettle full of hot cider. Is anyone interested?" She had to quickly add: "Settle down or you'll be at the back of the line!"

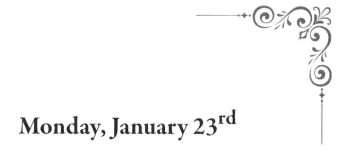

Monday, January 23rd

CHIEF PETROVIC LIKED to start the week with a meeting every Monday morning at 9 o'clock. He thought that having a meeting was a good idea for several reasons: it brought everybody together before the start of the next week; it helped develop camaraderie; it was an opportunity to summarize what had happened the previous week; and it was an opportunity to discuss any problems that had arisen.

This week, there was a lot to discuss. Cst. Herman was at our meeting, to everyone's delight. This was his first day back at work. Chief Petrovic had told him he was only working nine to noon this week. The chief would check with Peter at the end of the week to see how he was feeling.

"The first item on our agenda today is to discuss how we can be better prepared to conduct extensive property searches," said Chief Petrovic. "We need to realize we are unfamiliar with these properties, and that we need to conduct the search in a serious frame of mind. I know when you arrive at a farm, and you know you already have permission to search the property, you anticipate it will be a long and possibly boring chore. You don't see any dangerous aspect to it at all. I guess the lesson we learned this past week is that we must always be prepared, as best we can, for anything that may happen.

"So, once this meeting is over, I want the four of you to remain at this table to prepare a list of all the things you think we should carry with us when we embark on a property search. I think we were somewhat prepared, but I think you will find some things that should be

47

added to our knapsacks. We were fortunate the other day that Joel's fiancée Georgie is such a tenacious young woman. If she hadn't insisted, in such a determined manner, that we instigate a search immediately the outcome could've been tragic. I'll let you know right now, Joel, she can really get on your case."

Everyone laughed at that.

"I know that, from now on, I will not leave my office until the search team has reported in," continued the chief. "Further – and this is not a rebuke to Joel and Peter – take your guns with you. Not only can they be used for protection, but they can be used to signal for help."

The chief then turned to Peter and said, "Cst. Herman wanted to speak at this meeting."

Cst. Herman was very emotional and had difficulty speaking. "Joel is a great partner," he started. "When I needed him, he was there. Without his help I would be dead. He took me to shelter, he got a fire going, and he encouraged me as much as he could." Cst. Herman had to stop to get control of himself. Then he continued. "I also owe my life to you, Chief Petrovic, for getting the search party going, and for having Dr. Fitzgerald at the Conrad home. I am also indebted to Cst. Jarvis, Cst. Smith, Joel's dad, and Roger Conrad for getting me back to the Conrad farm house. The Conrads' hospitality to me and my wife while I was recovering was much appreciated." Cst. Herman had to sit down. He had desperately wanted to say the words he had spoken but now he could say no more.

There was silence for a minute or two.

"Thank you very much, Cst. Herman," said Chief Petrovic. "I'm proud of you and proud of this team." After a pause the chief continued. "There is one other item on this morning's agenda. Let me explain the good idea that Cst. Herman has come up with. Cst. Herman is going to be spending his mornings at the land registry office in the County Courthouse here in Chaseford for the remainder of this week, and for longer if necessary. Cst. Herman has talked to Stan Harris, who was in charge of the local tax records for forty years until his retirement last year. Stan is an encyclopedia of knowledge about property records, current and past owners, and changes that occurred to those properties. He has agreed to help Cst. Herman prepare a list of all those people who owned the farm properties we are interested in prior to the current owners. To start with, the list will go back thirty years. We are still not certain how old the body parts are, but we know they are not recent.

"The rest of us will continue with our searches. But the next search will not take place until next Monday at the earliest, weather providing. For the next month, or until I'm convinced Peter is well enough to search, I will assign the search teams. There will still be two constables on a team, but the twosome will rotate and there will always be one constable on duty in town.

"This meeting is over. There will be a break for pie and tea and then you are to carry on with your duties."

I WENT OVER TO GEORGIE'S parents' house for supper. The Harkness family lived on Durham Street, just a block or so from where my parents lived. They were really excited about our engagement. Georgie is the only girl in the family. She's a nurse at the local hospital, and her parents are very proud of her. I told them the details of the near tragedy at the Conrad farm, including Georgie's role in getting the search underway, and that made them even prouder.

"She's always been a very determined girl," her dad said. "Somehow, without being pushy, she always gets her way."

Her mother smiled and added, "As long as you do what you're told Joel, there will be no problems."

"That's enough mother," said Georgie, turning pink.

I had always gotten along really well with Mr. and Mrs. Harkness. We had a very pleasant meal. When we had finished helping with the dishes, Georgie and I headed back to my room at Franklin's Groceries.

Once we were alone in my apartment, we talked again about the events surrounding the rescue of Cst. Herman at the Conrad farm.

"When you first told me about your connection with Walter I didn't know whether to believe you or not," said Georgie. "I was pretty sure you weren't crazy, but it was a really weird idea. I guess I have to believe you now. I still don't know who that woman was that knocked on my parents' door. When my father answered it, she just handed him an envelope with my name on it and turned and left before he could say anything. She was tightly bundled up because of the heavy snow, so we never really got a look at her. My dad handed me the envelope and I read the note inside. It said:

> *"Walter says: Joel and Peter Herman are trapped at the back of the Conrad farm. Peter needs medical attention. Get people there as soon as you can.*

"I tried not to show any emotion because I didn't want my father connecting the woman to the emergency search that would follow. It would raise too many questions. I knew for certain it was an emergency because the note was from Walter, even if it was delivered by somebody else."

"Well, you certainly did a great job convincing Chief Petrovic that it was an emergency," I said.

"I had help," said Georgie. "I phoned Peter's wife before I phoned the chief. She was already upset. She called Chief Petrovic too. That convinced him to act. Don't worry. Your secret is still safe with me."

"I'm really glad it worked out," I said. "Something else very positive came out of this situation. I still don't know the identity of the mystery person, but I did get a note dropped off at my door. The note said:

> *"I'm glad I could help. It's great to know that someone else has the same ability I have. Perhaps in the future you will have to return the favour."*

I turned to Georgie and said, "We discovered a way to communicate through Walter. That could be important at some point in the future."

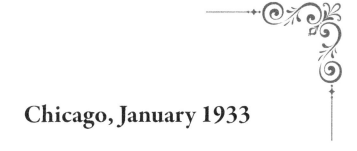

Chicago, January 1933

NEW YEAR'S WAS OVER and Johnnie Polizzi was counting his money. He was a big fan of Prohibition. It had made him a wealthy man. But as a regular reader of the Chicago Tribune he could see the writing on the wall and knew that sometime this year Prohibition would end. Without Prohibition he wouldn't make the kind of money he was used to.

When Capone had been running the show, things had been better. At the apex of Al Capone's Chicago career, he had had Mayor William Hill Thompson and the city police on his payroll. Polizzi had worked for Capone. The illegal distillery business had been a great money-maker. Then the FBI and Eliot Ness had interfered. Capone had been locked up in 1932, and that's when things started to get a lot more difficult for Johnnie Polizzi.

The new boss in town, Tony Accardo, was solidifying his organization and he had no room for Johnnie Polizzi. You could say that Johnnie Polizzi was an endangered species. Johnnie had a couple of men of his own for protection, but he knew he had to get out of Chicago if he wanted to live his natural lifespan. He and his lifelong friend Ernie Stanzio had had long talks about this. Their world had changed. New laws and an increasingly aggressive and powerful FBI were making it more difficult to earn a big income through illegitimate enterprise. Johnnie and Ernie realized they had two choices. They knew they had to leave Chicago for reasons of personal health. One choice was to move to another large city and try to connect with the crime boss there;

the other was to become legitimate businessmen. Being in their 40s, and heading towards 50, they decided to look for legitimate business opportunities far away from Chicago.

One day, as they were having their lunch, Ernie said, "I've got relatives in this place called Hamilton, Ontario. It's in Canada, you know."

"I know that," said Johnnie. "You and I have been to Ontario at least three times. But it has been a while. Don't you remember when we were young guys, in 1911, and I bought that fancy Stanley Touring car? We just decided one day to drive to Ontario and visit that girl we'd met in Chicago. Her parents had sent her to DePaul University, remember?"

"I kind of forgot," said Ernie. "My brother Beno has been pestering me to come visit him. He says Hamilton's a nice quiet town. It's not dangerous like Chicago. My niece is getting married on January 28th. I'm seriously considering going. My brother would be glad to see you too. Why don't you come with me? That would be a great place to find a legitimate business opportunity."

Johnnie thought for a moment and then said, "Okay, I'll go. Do I need to pack snowshoes?"

"Not for the 'Steel City' you don't," answered Ernie, laughing.

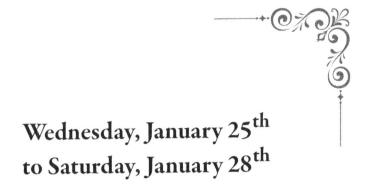

Wednesday, January 25th to Saturday, January 28th

JOHNNIE AND ERNIE TOOK the early train out of Chicago on Wednesday morning. They had run their betting operation out of a storefront and had lived in an apartment above the store. It wasn't fancy.

They left no loose ends. With one thing and another, their wives and families had left them long ago. One of Johnnie's sons still dropped by regularly, though. Johnnie told him he was going out of town and that, once things were settled down, he would let him know where he was. He wasn't going to leave any clues behind about his destination for Tony Accardo to follow.

They had to switch trains in Detroit. They boarded a train that ran from Detroit to Toronto with many stops along the way. They would be getting off at the station in Hamilton. Ernie's brother, Beno, said either he or someone that worked for him would pick them up at the station and take them to his house. The trip was uneventful. Sure enough, late Thursday afternoon, when they arrived at the station in Hamilton, Ernie's brother Beno was there to pick them up.

Ernie introduced his partner and pal, Johnnie, to Beno.

"I'm thrilled to meet ya," said Beno. "Ernie tells me you're a great man, Johnnie. He says you've paid him well and protected him. And since you're both coming out of Chicago alive, it must be true. Just throw your luggage and your bags of money in the back of my car and we'll head home."

"This is a pretty nice car you have, Beno," said Johnnie. "It's one of those new Chrysler Airflows isn't it?"

"It is," said Beno. "I like the design. It looks a little different, but the engineering's great. My future son-in-law sold it to me. Why don't you sit up at the front with me? Ernie can sit in the back and guard the money."

It didn't take long to get to Beno Stanzio's home, a substantial house on a large lot. Off to the side was a three-car garage with an apartment above.

"Brother, you've done very well," said Ernie. "I didn't know you had an estate."

"The construction business has been good to me," his brother answered with a wink.

Johnnie and Ernie were staying in the apartment above the garage. That would give them some privacy. When they went into the house for dinner there were women everywhere. There were mothers and grandmothers and daughters, all in a great swirl of excitement about the wedding on Saturday.

THE MOST BLESSED SACRAMENT Roman Catholic Church in Hamilton was packed to overflowing. The wedding was a great occasion. A grand reception was held at Beno Stanzio's home and Johnnie and Ernie had a good time. After the reception was over, Beno invited Johnnie and Ernie to meet with him in his den.

When they entered the den there was another, older gentleman there. Johnnie recognized him as the groom's father.

"Let me introduce Carlo Mossa," said Beno. When the introductions were completed, Beno started the conversation by saying: "I've been talking with Johnnie and my brother Ernie and they've indicated they may be interested in purchasing a business in Canada. They want something that's not too big and that's easy to operate. I immediately thought of your hardware business, Carlo. I know your business does well and that you have an excellent staff. Your son has told me you're thinking of selling and retiring. I hope I'm not speaking out of turn."

"Not at all," said Carlo. "We are like family now. It's okay for you to know my plans."

The negotiations began and, with Beno acting as an intermediary, they were successfully concluded within a week. Johnnie Polizzi and Ernie Stanzio would become the owners of a hardware business in Hamilton.

According to Carlo, the business would run itself. Under the terms of the agreement, Carlo would supervise the business until Polizzi and Stanzio took over officially on March 31.

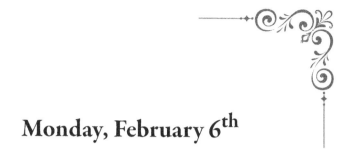

Monday, February 6th

IT WAS ANOTHER 9 O'CLOCK Monday morning meeting in the chief's office. We were in the heart of winter and we were still searching farms.

"I thought I'd cheer you guys up today," said Chief Petrovic. "Do you remember the news from last Thursday?"

When we all gave the chief a blank stare he said, "According to the radio, when Punxsutawney Phil emerged from his home on Gobbler's Knob two miles southeast of Punxsutawney, Pennsylvania, last Thursday he saw his shadow."

We all groaned. That meant six more weeks of winter and six more weeks of difficult searches.

It had been two and a half weeks since the trouble on Conrad's farm. The doctor and Chief Petrovic had both given Cst. Herman the green light to return to his regular duties. When that was announced at the start of today's meeting everyone cheered. Cst. Herman had a smile on his face that would glow in the dark.

The farm searches had continued as the weather would permit. There had been no more misadventures. Everyone had heard about Cst. Herman's brush with death and the cooperation and welcome we received when we visited the farms to search was outstanding.

"I'll turn the meeting over the Cst. Herman so he can give you a report on what he and Stan Harris have been doing at the land registry office," said Chief Petrovic.

"I know where Stan and I have been searching is a lot warmer than where you have been searching," said Cst. Herman.

"I hope you're not teasing us," said Cst. Jay Jarvis.

"No, I'm just having some fun," said Cst. Herman, grinning.

"Back to the report please," said the chief with a smile.

Cst. Herman continued. "It's a boring process to search titles, but every now and then, especially with Stan's help, I learn something new. We've been averaging about four thorough property searches a day, so we're almost halfway through the farms in the area that Jay's map targeted.

"Quite a number of properties have changed hands. But many of those went from father to son, or, on occasion, father to daughter. There have also been some new buildings erected in the past thirty years but not as many as you would think. The older buildings were not usually torn down, although sometimes they were partially dismantled to supply wood or timbers for a new building. In this area, it seems people are more liable to try and fix the building they have than build a new one.

"During our search, to date, Stan and I noted three farms that currently, or in the past, had abattoirs. We think they deserve extra attention. We've also found two occasions where farm houses were destroyed by fire. One of those is of special interest to Stan and me. It's the Featherstone farm."

"I know that story," interjected the chief. "I was a young man and had just started my career as a constable. It must be over twenty years since the fire. There was a very large home on that farm. At the time it may have been the biggest house in the county. The Featherstones were very well-to-do. Then tragedy struck. Late one fall evening, the large farmhouse was destroyed in a fire.

"When the fire site had cooled down and we were able to look through the debris we found only one body. It appeared to be a young female. It was likely the body of Nancy Featherstone. She was their youngest and only child and lived in the house with them. She would have been about twenty when she died. So far as the neighbours knew, Nancy and her mom and dad were the only ones in the house. Since that time, her parents have never been seen."

"Stan and I were able to dig up the following information," said Cst. Herman. "The spring after the fire, Mr. Featherstone's brother William took over responsibility for the farm. He was the only living relative that could be found. Over the next several years, other farmers worked the land. They split the profits from the land with William Featherstone and that money went into the Featherstone estate. Then seven years after the fire the courts declared the Featherstones dead in absentia. The estate, including the farm, passed on to William Featherstone. He died a couple of years ago. His son Henry now has title to the farm."

"I think, from what you just heard from Cst. Herman, the search at the land registry office has not been a waste of time," said Chief Petrovic. "So for a few days we are going to change the focus of the farm searches. Peter will continue working with Stan, searching titles only in the mornings. In the afternoons, he will be on regular duties, helping me and answering local police calls as required. You other three will continue with the farm searches. But for the next few days you are to concentrate on the three farms with abattoirs and on the two farms where fires have destroyed houses."

The rest of us could see from Cst. Herman's face that he was very disappointed that he would not be going out on farm searches yet.

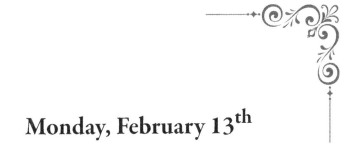

Monday, February 13th

"LET'S HEAR YOUR REPORTS," said Chief Petrovic. "I'll start with Cst. Herman. He doesn't seem to be happy with what he's accomplished this past week."

"He has been grumpy," said Cst. Smith.

"I'm just disappointed with myself," said Cst. Herman. "Stan and I haven't found anything new at the registry office and I miss being part of the team out on the farm searches."

"That sounds like your report," said Chief Petrovic.

Cst. Herman smiled and said, "It was. I basically have nothing to report."

"Who wants to go to next?" asked the chief.

"I'll give you the abattoir report," said Jay. "It's very similar to Peter's report. However, a bit of explanation might be helpful. Not only did we do the abattoirs, but we did the attached farms as well. We quickly realized that so much blood has been shed in those abattoirs that we will never be able to determine anything that happened years ago, and probably not even a month ago. It's a dead end."

"Do you other fellows share Jay's conclusion?" asked the chief.

Cst. Smith and I nodded in agreement.

It was my turn next. Cst. Smith and I had drawn the duty of searching the Featherstone farm. Everyone looked at me, hoping my report would be more interesting than the previous two reports.

It would be. Cst. Jake Smith and I had been out to the Featherstone farm Friday afternoon. We had not started on the land yet, but we had taken a look at what remained of the house. We also had time to look at the other outbuildings. They were still intact and being used. Only the large home had been destroyed by the fire. When we returned to the chief's office late Friday afternoon, we had a brief discussion with Chief Petrovic about what we had found on the site. The chief was already aware of what I was going to report.

"Jake and I were unable to complete the search of the buildings and the land on Friday," I said. "However, we did have time to take a look at what was left of the house. There's not much there. The place burned down in 1911. Time and the weather have not improved the site. It was quickly apparent to us that we would not learn anything new from what was left of the home. So we started on the outbuildings. They are still in use. I think anything out of place in those outbuildings would've been noticed and immediately reported to us. To be thorough, Jake and I did the inspection and saw nothing of interest.

"We were getting ready to leave when Jake noticed there was a bit of a rise in the land about fifty yards behind the house. He said to me: 'That doesn't look like a natural hill. It looks like someone has artificially piled up earth there. And it's not a ramp because it's not going anywhere. Seems out of place to me. Let's go take a look.' I followed Jake over to the mound.

"We were both surprised by what we found. It wasn't just a pile of earth. When we got close to it we could see that it was a small, cabin-like structure with a door on the east side. We couldn't get the door open because there is quite a bit of earth in front of it. It will take a great deal of shoveling to get into that small building. I had never seen anything like it before, but Jake said his grandpa had something like it on his farm. Jake said his grandpa used it for cold storage. So we decided to take a walk around the building before we left for the day. Jake take over."

Cst. Jake Smith cleared his throat and said, "When we got around to the other side of the structure, we noticed some large animal had dug a hole to get to the wall of the building. The wall was made of wood, and there was a hole in the wall. We could see very little from where we were, but we could see ice inside. Joel and I also noticed lots of tracks leading from that hole out across the fields. They looked like dog tracks to us. It was getting close to five and almost dark, so we headed back to town and reported in to the chief."

Chief Petrovic looked around. He could tell everyone was excited. He could tell they could hardly wait to get back to the Featherstone farm to continue the search.

"Tomorrow is a special day," said the Chief Petrovic. "All of us are going to practice the art of digging. It won't be easy to clear the dirt away from the door of that structure. It's winter, and the ground is frozen, so we will need to use picks, most likely. We will meet here at 9 o'clock tomorrow morning. I want you all to bring a shovel and a pick and bring the gear that we usually take on a farm search. If we don't finish by noon we will stop for lunch and go to Mabel's diner. I'll pay."

GEORGIE AND I HAD BEEN invited to Gwen Cummings's home for supper. This was a total surprise to us. We didn't know Gwen Cummings but we were curious. Our invitation had included Gwen's address and had ended with her signature and the notation 'a secret admirer'. She lived on the southern edge of Chaseford in a modest story-and-a-half home.

The woman that opened the door was petite. She had curly hair and Georgie told me later she had guessed her to be in her early 50s. Gwen welcomed us in. She had us hang up our coats and hats and take off our winter boots.

"I wasn't sure whether to contact you or not," she said. "You know I have lived with my secret for a long time. I wasn't sure I wanted to share it with anyone. I have made an effort to find out a bit about both of you. From idle conversation with people I know, and even from the nice gentleman who runs the store where I buy groceries." She smiled at me when she said that. "I felt very confident about inviting you to my home after listening to what people had to say about each of you."

While she was talking, Georgie and I looked at each other with a knowing glance. We were quite certain we knew who Gwen Cummings was.

She smiled at us and said, "Yes, I'm that other person that has the same special ability that you have, Joel. I am Gwen Cummings and I'm very pleased to meet you and Georgie. When you both went to such lengths to protect my privacy during the crisis with Cst. Herman, and then didn't attempt to locate me afterward, I knew you were people I could trust. Living with a secret isn't easy."

I nodded in agreement.

"I've had this talent for as long as I can remember," she continued. "When I was young, my parents attributed my comments to a vivid imagination. But as I became a teenager, I realized I couldn't let anyone know that I could contact someone they couldn't see. As a result, it's limited my friendships and I've never married.

"I wanted to have this meeting so that I could learn more about both of you and about Joel's abilities. I also wanted to know about your contact, Joel, and I thought I would tell you about my contact. I thought it was also necessary to include Georgie as well. I know you don't have our ability, Georgie, but you know about us and you don't think we're crazy. So you are someone else we can both talk to.

"But let's have supper. We can start our conversation while we're eating. I prepared a chicken dinner with mashed potatoes, some carrots from the cold cellar, and some of my special pickled beets. I baked a chocolate cake for dessert. I heard somewhere that it was Joel's favourite dessert."

We sat at the table and as we ate we talked.

"I think I was born with this special ability," said Gwen. "From listening to my dad talk about his mother, I think she may have had this ability too. Many people thought grandma was just a bit strange."

"I'm the first one in our family to have this kind of ability," I said. "I wasn't born with this power to communicate with a deceased person. I was struck by lightning during the big storm of 1928. That stimulated something in my brain and immediately gave me this talent."

"That was a terrible storm," said Gwen. "I was fortunate I was out of town that weekend, visiting my aunt Agatha in London. But when I came back to Chaseford late Sunday evening I was upset by all the destruction I saw.

"The human brain must naturally have the capacity to do this kind of communication," said Gwen. "I can understand inheriting the ability, but when you suffered electrical trauma and could then communicate this way it implies to me that everyone must have this latent potential."

"I think it's a possibility," I said, "but I'm not certain we'll find a volunteer who's willing to get struck by lightning to test out the theory."

We all laughed.

"Let's leave that for now. I want to tell you about my contact," said Gwen.

At this point I interrupted and said, "My contact Walter and I use the word 'essence.'"

"I like that word," said Gwen. "My contact's name is Floyd. He lived in the house next door. The end of his life was a tragedy. It ended horrifically."

Gwen told us she had not had many adventures with Floyd until she became an important part in the rescue of Cst. Herman from the Conrad farm. Until then, the most significant event that had occurred happened when her parents' home caught fire and Floyd woke her so that she was able to alert her parents. The fire department put out the blaze without much damage.

I told Gwen all about Walter's and my involvement in bringing justice to Louise Carter after she was murdered. This, of course, was a surprise to Gwen but she was really pleased and excited that someone like me or her, with this special ability, had been so helpful.

"I sometimes wondered if my gift was a curse that set me apart from other people," said Gwen. "But now that I've been involved in a situation where a life was saved, and I've learned of another case where justice was served, I feel much more comfortable with myself.

"I've done a lot of reading and thinking about having an ability that is not ordinary," she said. "I certainly don't believe some of the claims by people like Edgar Cayce, but I do believe that I'm different and that you are different, Joel. I also believe that, just as one's language skills can improve, our unique ability may be capable of growth."

Georgie and I looked at her. "I'm not sure what you mean," I said. "I think you will have to explain to me what you are after."

"Do you know what telepathy is?" she asked.

The three of us spent the rest of the evening debating whether or not telepathy was possible and how we could go about conducting experiments to see if it was.

Tuesday, February 14th

IT WAS ONE OF THOSE bright, cold, calm February days. The sky was a robin's egg blue and the bright sun, although not yet high in the sky, seemed to give everything a sharp outline. The five of us had arrived at the Featherstone farm at about 9:30. Chief Petrovic and Cst. Herman had driven out in the Ford Radio Motor Patrol car. Jay and I had been driven to the Featherstone farm by Cst. Smith in the 1932 Ford pickup truck. The police department was fortunate to have the truck. It had been donated by a wealthy local merchant and proved to be useful from time to time. Today we had a large sled in the back as well as our picks and shovels and some large burlap bags.

We got out of our vehicles and carried our picks and shovels over to the mysterious mound. From the distance it looked like a huge snow-drift, but when you got close to it you could easily make out the cabin-like structure, almost hidden under the snow.

We did one complete circuit of the cabin, noting the hole in the back wall and the disturbances in the snow created by animal activity. The building appeared to be about 10 feet wide and 14 feet long. It had a slanted roof, and the low side wall facing the house was about 6 feet tall. The other wall, furthest from the house, appeared to be about 8 feet tall. It was easy to understand that, once the snow had blown in around it, and with the short wall closest to the back of the house, it could easily be mistaken for a snowdrift if you didn't take a closer look.

We returned to the front of the building to examine the partially buried door. There was quite a bit of earth in front of it and the dirt appeared to have been there for many years. That helped to explain why no one had bothered with the building. It would take considerable time and effort to clear the earth away. With Chief Petrovic in the role of supervisor, we set to work with our picks and shovels. There was only enough room for one of us to work at a time. That was good, because even in the frigid weather the man with the pick quickly worked up a sweat and tired himself out. The earth was frozen hard and the picks got a good workout.

In a little over an hour we had the area in front of the door cleaned out and had amassed a respectable pile of dirt. The chief stepped forward to open the door. It wouldn't open. That, in itself, was not a surprise. It probably had not been opened for many years.

Chief Petrovic turned to Cst. Smith and said: "Hand me your pick."

Just before the chief swung the pick, Cst. Jay Jarvis said, "Shouldn't you knock first?"

For some reason, we all found that really funny. Everyone burst into laughter. Well, everyone but the chief.

All Chief Petrovic said was, "Jay, I see a lot of unpleasant duties ahead of you."

The door splintered easily on the first blow. The chief and Cst. Herman removed most of the pieces of the door and tossed them in a second pile out of the way in the snow. Chief Petrovic said, "Joel, light the kerosene lantern and hand it to me, please."

I lit the lantern and passed it to Chief Petrovic. He stepped through the opening and we heard him exclaim, "For heaven sakes, this is an ice house."

I had not been in an ice house before. The iceman had always delivered ice for our icebox at home and ice for the freezer ice boxes at our grocery store. I had watched him come along the street, with his team of horses pulling a big wagon full of large blocks of ice. I even talked to the iceman a couple of times. I was surprised at how easily he used those large tongs to move the ice from his wagon to whatever icebox he was going to. I knew there was a large storage shed in town full of ice blocks, but I had never given much thought to how ice got to the farms. I don't think every farm had an ice house, but the Featherstones had been very well off.

We followed Chief Petrovic through the door, but he had stopped rather suddenly and the rest of us found ourselves crowded together just inside. The light from the kerosene lamp reflecting from the contents of the building produced an eerie effect. There were still a great many blocks of ice stored in this structure, though it wasn't as full as it would have been when they had first packed the ice in. We stood there and stared. This was not what we had expected.

Suddenly Cst. Herman pointed, and, in a voice more high-pitched than usual, said, "I think that's a body back in the corner."

It was.

"Jay, go back out to the truck and bring the sled," said the chief. "We're going to need it."

As the chief moved cautiously along the side aisle towards the back of the icehouse we heard a loud growl.

"Don't worry, it's just a German shepherd," said the chief, "and I've got my pick." He swung the pick menacingly and the dog turned and quickly scampered out the hole in the back of the ice house.

There was a narrow space along the rear wall of the building where we found an assortment of body parts scattered about. It was a grisly scene, though it was obvious that the remains had been there a long time. Because of the cold temperature in the ice house, and the time that had passed, there wasn't much of an odour, but the appearance of severed chunks of human bodies caused all of us to feel nauseated.

Jay came back with the sled and we loaded it up with burlap bags containing two torsos, two arms, two legs and a head.

"If you add what we found today to what we've recovered previously, I think the total is two bodies," said the chief. There was a grim expression on his face. "The forensics lab in Toronto will have to give us confirmation, but I strongly suspect that we may have recovered the bodies of Mr. and Mrs. Featherstone. Right now, it appears that they were murdered and dismembered. I also strongly suspect that the house fire was arson. Because of the amount of time that's elapsed, this probably will be a lengthy and difficult investigation.

"For the time being, I think we'll try to conduct this investigation without the aid of the London police force. Cst. Smith and Cst. Herman gained a lot of valuable experience and proved their worth in the investigation of Louise Carter's murder.

"Let's get the truck loaded and get back to town so we can deliver these body parts to Dr. Whittles."

Wednesday, February 22nd

CHIEF PETROVIC HAD postponed his Monday morning meeting until Wednesday. He said Dr. Whittles had told him that the forensics people in Toronto would likely get a report back to him on the body parts by Tuesday afternoon at the latest. Farm searches had been postponed for the time being. With the discovery of the body parts in the icehouse on the Featherstone farm, and the subsequent story in the local paper, people living in the area of Chaseford and the surrounding countryside had been put at ease. Even though it had been made clear to the public previously that the body parts discovered earlier were from many years ago, the public had still felt somewhat threatened. Now they could relax.

Chief Petrovic started the meeting by discussing the report that he'd received via Dr. Whittles from the forensics lab in Toronto. He said that, to the best of their knowledge, the forensic pathologists concluded that all the body parts came from only two bodies. Analysis indicated that one body was that of an older male, and the other body was that of an older female. They were unable to determine the ages exactly. There was also no way to determine with any certainty that the bodies were those of Mr. and Mrs. Featherstone.

With the forensic report out of the way, the chief carried on with his second item. "You will recall, previously, that I mentioned as a young police constable I had visited the site of the Featherstone fire. After the events of last week, I'm convinced that not only was the fire set deliberately, but that most likely it was set because it was a crime scene. I think the murders and the subsequent cutting up of the bodies took place in that house.

"As you know, Cst. Jarvis has been working with me these past few days, going back over old records. We have been reviewing all local police reports, focusing on any complaints the public made about feeling threatened from January 1st, 1911, up to the date of the fire on October 3, 1911. We think we've found something. I'll let Jay tell you about it."

"On Labor Day, September 4, 1911," said Cst. Jay Jarvis, "there was an incident at the Featherstone farm. The local police had to be called to ask two young gentlemen to leave."

"Were you one of the constables that went to the farm that day, Chief?" asked Cst. Herman.

"No, I was at a Labor Day picnic that day," said the chief. "Please continue, Jay."

"According to the report, two young Americans, Johnnie Polizzi and Ernie Stanzio, had driven their fancy new car all the way from Chicago to visit Nancy Featherstone. It turns out that they told her parents they would deliver Nancy back to DePaul University for the next term. Mr. Featherstone told them Nancy wasn't going back to DePaul the following year. He told them to leave the property immediately. There was a lot of shouting and screaming from everyone, including Nancy.

"One of the neighbours happened to be going by in their buggy and saw that there was a ruckus. They took their buggy straight into Chaseford to get the police. Once the police arrived, the two young fellows got into their vehicle and left. Mr. Featherstone declined to press charges since the two fellows left promptly. The two young fellows never returned to the area and as a result the incident was never followed up on."

"Now it's time to follow up on this incident," said Chief Petrovic. "I think it's a lead worth pursuing. Cst. Jarvis has already volunteered to go to Chicago."

The last comment caught everyone's attention. No one could remember the last time a Chaseford policeman got to go on a trip.

"Don't look so stunned," said the chief. "Just my little joke. Nobody's going to Chicago. Thank heavens for the invention of the telephone. I had a feeling these young men might be known to the Chicago police, so I contacted the Chicago Police Department.

"The police in Chicago told me Polizzi and Stanzio were a couple of small-time hoodlums. They seem to have left Chicago very suddenly within the last month. No one knows where they went. The police lieutenant I was talking to told me one of the mob guys, Tony Accardo, was after them. He said they were either out of the area or at the bottom of Lake Michigan. He didn't care. He just didn't want them back in Chicago. The lieutenant told me Johnnie Polizzi still has some family in Chicago. His one son seems somewhat close to Johnnie. He told me he is a good young man and that he would check with the son sometime this week and get back to me. The lieutenant figures Johnnie's son is the only one in Chicago who will know where Johnnie and Ernie went if they're still alive.

"Until we get some more information, we are temporarily stalled in the investigation. But we have lots of other work to do in town, so you'd better go and look after it."

IT WAS MY TURN TO PLAY the host. Tonight, Georgie and Gwen Cummings were coming to my one-room apartment at the back of the store for a late supper. My dad knew I had company there now and then, but my parents didn't mind; after all, I had sacrificed my room at 200 Durham Street to Granny Watson. Unfortunately, all I had to cook with was a hot plate, and it was only good for warming things up. So, for fancy meals like this, I had to rely on my mom and my grandma. They prepared an extra-large supper, and right after they ate my brother Ralph, my sister Emmylou, and my dad packed what was left from the meal in the car and brought it down to the store. Tonight, there was even a fresh-baked chocolate cake.

The timing was great. My family had only been gone about five minutes when Georgie arrived, quickly followed by Gwen Cummings. They both smiled and said things like "Oh, you shouldn't have gone to all this trouble." Then Georgie spoiled it all by saying, "Please thank your mom and grandma the first chance you get."

Both of them burst into laughter.

"Let's eat, it looks delicious," said Gwen, finally.

When we'd finished our meal, Georgie said, "You don't have a very good place to wash this many dishes."

"I know, just leave them for now," I said. "I'll take care them later. Let's talk about telepathy."

The three of us had been doing some reading since we'd talked about the possibility of telepathy the first time a week or so ago at Gwen's house. I don't think we really knew much more about telepathy after doing the reading, but we were still quite interested to see whether it was possible for Gwen and me to communicate telepathically because of the unique ability we shared. And I had the perfect lab. Since one wall of my apartment was nothing but a stack of boxes, a person could just walk around the stack and they would be out of sight.

Our amateur scientific explanation was based on the hypothesis that, if you focused your mind, you could project some kind of electromagnetic signal. Walter and I were convinced that that was how we communicated. Perhaps Gwen's mind and my mind had developed the ability to perform this type of broadcast in a minor way.

Tonight's parlour game would require a deck of playing cards. To begin with, Georgie and Gwen would go to the other side of the wall. Georgie, who would be holding the deck of cards, would randomly draw one from the deck, take a look at it, and show it to Gwen. Georgie would say 'ready' loud enough for me to hear on the other side of the wall. I would pick up my pencil and get ready to write down the name of the card on my pad of paper. Gwen would concentrate intently on the card in her hand for a moment, then she would nod at Georgie and Georgie would say 'finished'. This would be repeated for three different cards, then the three of us would meet together to take a look at what I had written down.

At the end of the first session, when we took a look at my answers, I had identified one of the three cards correctly. I was disappointed, but 33% was still somewhat impressive. I thought that, since I had to write down not only the value of the card but also the suit, I only had one chance in 52 of being correct if the results were truly random.

Then Georgie asked me a very good question. "I know Gwen was concentrating, because I was there, but were you concentrating as you would if you were listening intently for something, or were you just hoping something would come into your mind?"

"I confess, I probably wasn't concentrating as much as I should," I said.

"That's pretty much what I figured," Georgie said with a smile.

We tried the experiment again. This time I went to the other side of the wall with Georgie while Gwen stayed behind with the paper and pencil. When we got together this time the results were more impressive. Gwen had guessed two of the cards correctly and was only out slightly on the third one. She'd written down 'two of clubs' instead of 'three of clubs'.

"I don't know how to explain this," said Gwen, "but when I was concentrating, I thought I almost felt something."

We tried the experiment four more times. At the end of the night, Gwen and I had each had a chance to predict nine cards correctly. Gwen had predicted seven out of the nine and I had predicted six out of the nine correctly. That was a total of 13 out of 18 correct guesses. By my calculations, that was a success rate of over 70%. It certainly wasn't random.

We'd had a lot of fun and we were excited. We may have found something out. Georgie suggested another good test.

"Why not have two people that don't share your ability try the same test?"

"You're so clever, Georgie," I said. "And beautiful too."

Georgie blushed and Gwen laughed. The compliment was worth it; Georgie stayed and helped me with the dishes.

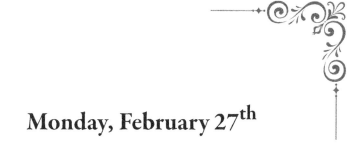

Monday, February 27th

IT WAS MONDAY MORNING again and the chief had us gathered around the table in his office.

"Just before we get down to business, I have one question to ask Joel," said the chief.

The serious look on Chief Petrovic's face had me worried. I had no idea where this was going.

Chief Petrovic grinned and said, "Joel, what's this rumour I was hearing this morning at Mabel's Diner? Is it true about your brother Ralph? Everyone in Chaseford and area knows he's the best ballplayer around. He's a heck of a third baseman. Someone at breakfast this morning said Ralph has been invited for a tryout with the Cleveland Indians. If he's successful, he would likely end up on the Butler Indians roster in the Pennsylvania State Association."

Spring training is just around the corner. Baseball talk is already heating up at the diner. The Detroit Tiger fans are still stirred up. They don't seem to realize that the Cardinals beat them in the World Series last year, four games to three. A lot of us at the diner are Cleveland Indian fans. Cleveland had a good team last year too. The Indians finished third in the American League. There's a lot of joking – and a lot of insults – being tossed around in the diner by fans of both teams. Mabel has already warned us: "If anybody starts a food fight, they'll be gone for a month. But not until after they clean up the mess."

"That rumour is true," I said. "My brother Ralph got a letter from the Cleveland Indians organization last Thursday. My mother gave it to him at the supper table. There was so much whooping and hollering my mother sent him and my dad outside to cool off. We are all really excited. We know Ralph has a special talent for baseball. So far, the only thing that's certain is the tryout. But the entire family is convinced he'll be successful. But I know my mom won't let him join a minor league team until he finishes his school year. She thinks he's too young to be going somewhere else to play baseball. If he gets a contract offer – and I think he will – it will be up to Ralph and my dad to convince my mom that it's okay for Ralph to go to the states and play ball for the summer."

As soon as I'd finished talking the other constables made almost as much noise as my dad and Ralph had made Thursday evening.

"Now to other business," said the chief. "I did hear back from the police lieutenant in Chicago. He talked to Johnnie Polizzi's son. The young man told him he'd received a letter from his dad saying he could make contact with Johnnie by getting in touch with Beno Stanzio in Hamilton, Ontario. I don't know who was more surprised about Polizzi being in Ontario, the Chicago lieutenant or myself.

"I followed up on that lead by contacting the chief of police in Hamilton, hoping that Beno Stanzio was known to the police there. The Hamilton chief of police does know him. He said he knows nothing about him ever being involved in any criminal activity, but the chief and Beno Stanzio both attend the Most Blessed Sacrament Roman Catholic Church in Hamilton. As a matter of fact, the Hamilton chief of police attended the wedding of Beno's daughter at the end of January. He said Beno is a very friendly and gregarious guy. He runs a large and successful construction company based in Hamilton. Beno's a Canadian citizen and has lived in Hamilton for well over twenty years. The chief of police considers himself a friend of Beno's and would have no trouble asking Beno about the whereabouts of Johnnie Polizzi. The chief said he hoped to be back to me before the end of the week. There appears to be little else we can do in this case until I hear back about the location of Johnnie Polizzi. Once we find Johnnie, I will set up an interview with him."

Shortly after that the meeting ended.

GEORGIE AND I WENT out to a fancy restaurant for supper. Actually, it was Mabel's Diner, but the food is always good and affordable. With the Depression still going on it was a rare meal out for us even though we are both employed now. We had a table to ourselves, and we were having a good meal and pleasant conversation until Proofie Duncan appeared and offered to serenade us for 25 cents. I think the idea was to pay him the quarter so he would go away without serenading you. Proofie was a little under the weather; it was obvious from his speech and behaviour that he'd been attacked by the demon alcohol. Mabel had him escorted to the door and beyond.

Georgie started a new conversation with, "I think we should invite Jay and Sylvia over to your place Friday evening. We could play some games and have some snacks. I was thinking of one game in particular." I still hadn't caught on, so Georgie said, "The game I was thinking of is the one that we played with Gwen Cummings."

This time the light went on. It wasn't real bright but at least it was on.

"Aha, this time we can work in a test involving two people that don't have the abilities that Gwen and I have."

"You're so smart, Joel," said Georgie. "We don't even need to let them know that we're running a test."

"I like your idea," I said. "Give Sylvia a call. I know her mom can hardly wait to look after Baby Brad."

Friday, March 3rd

LATE THURSDAY AFTERNOON, just before Chief Petrovic left his office, he received a phone call from the Hamilton police chief, Sam O'Donnell. Chief O'Donnell had phoned Chief Petrovic to inform him that his conversation with Beno Stanzio had been successful. O'Donnell had just received a call back from Beno. Beno had contacted his brother Ernie and Ernie's friend Johnnie Polizzi. They had agreed to meet Chief Petrovic at the Hamilton police station on Friday at a time convenient to the chief.

"Two o'clock in the afternoon would be a good time for me," said Chief Petrovic. "I'll bring one of my constables with me. It should take us a little under two hours to drive there. We'll have an early lunch and then head to Hamilton. I haven't been to your police station before, so perhaps you should give me some specific directions."

Chief Petrovic jotted down the directions, then he thanked Chief O'Donnell for locating Polizzi and Stanzio. Chief Petrovic was still amazed at what a coincidence it was that Chief O'Donnell knew Stanzio's brother Beno. The chief then contacted Cst. Herman.

"You're going on a field trip with me tomorrow. To the Steel City," he said.

"You can't fool me," said Cst. Herman. "I've been to Hamilton before and I know we wouldn't be driving to Pittsburgh."

Chief Petrovic and Cst. Herman arrived at the Hamilton police station about ten minutes before 2 o'clock. They were greeted by Chief

O'Donnell, who escorted them to an interview room. Chief O'Donnell told them that Beno and Ernie Stanzio and Johnnie Polizzi had arrived about ten minutes before them. When the Stanzios and Polizzi had arrived, Chief O'Donnell had escorted them to a different room. He didn't want them bumping into Chief Petrovic and Cst. Herman until Chief O'Donnell could make introductions.

"We would like to interview Johnnie Polizzi by himself, first," said Chief Petrovic.

"Okay, I'll go and get Johnnie. Ernie can stay and chat with his brother while Johnnie's being interviewed," said Chief O'Donnell.

In a couple of minutes, Chief O'Donnell returned with a man about 50 years old whom he introduced as Johnnie Polizzi. Polizzi was about 6 feet tall and a bit on the stocky side. He looked like he had probably been a decent athlete in his youth. He didn't seem alarmed to see them.

"How can I help you gentlemen?" he asked.

"We're just trying to clear up a situation that occurred a number of years ago," said Chief Petrovic. "You may have some information that could help us. We're also curious as to why you're in Canada now, and why you are so reluctant to give out your address?"

"My friend Ernie Stanzio and I are reluctant to give anyone our address," said Johnnie. "At the moment, we're in Canada on a six-month visitor's visa. We may want to stay longer. You can check with the police in Chicago. I don't think there are any warrants out on us. But we have come to the attention of a mob guy there named Tony Accardo. We don't know why he's taken a dislike to us, but we didn't feel safe in Chicago. We don't know if Mr. Accardo has friends in Canada or not but we don't want to meet them."

"I've read about Mr. Accardo in the newspaper," said Chief Petrovic. "You're probably wise to remain anonymous if you can. I'm going to ask you some questions about an event that happened over twenty years ago, near the town of Chaseford. I hope you have a good memory."

"I know I was young and foolish," said Johnnie, "but I don't remember doing anything that would have led to an arrest. I'm not even sure where Chaseford is."

"Maybe I can jog your memory," said Chief Petrovic. "Does the name Featherstone ring a bell? Remember this is from more than twenty years ago. Did you know anybody from Ontario name Featherstone?"

Chief Petrovic watched Johnnie Polizzi's face as it went from a blank look to a look that seemed to say: 'Oh yeah.'

"I guess from my reaction I did know somebody," said Johnnie. "I just wasn't quite sure of the last name. We always called her Nancy."

"So, would you agree that you knew someone called Nancy Featherstone back then?" asked the chief.

"Yeah, Ernie and I met her when she was going to school in Chicago. At DePaul University. That would've been 1910 or 1911. She was a very outgoing girl. She was beautiful and impulsive and liked to have things her own way. As long as you marched to her drumbeat, things were okay. If you crossed her, there was hell to pay. A lot of screaming and tossing of anything that was handy."

"How did you get to meet Nancy Featherstone?" asked Chief Petrovic. "I strongly suspect you weren't going to DePaul University at the time."

"No, Ernie and I were in our mid-20s. We liked to party. Nancy and her friends liked to party too. At that time, we were all using cocaine. You could still get cocaine from a druggist then if you had a prescription. Since one of the druggists often partied with us, that was no problem. I know the 1922 law put serious restrictions on using cocaine, but it wasn't illegal then, so I don't mind talking about it. I haven't used it much since."

"How did you end up at the Featherstone farm in September 1911?" asked Cst. Herman.

"I got a letter from Nancy," said Johnnie. "I doubt if I still have it. It would've been tossed long ago. But you can check with Ernie; he knows I got the letter. She knew I had a new Stanley Touring car and she wanted Ernie and me to drive from Chicago to her farm. We were supposed to take her some cocaine. It seemed to be scarce where she lived. Then we were all going to drive back to Chicago. We would drop her off at DePaul University in time for the start of her next school year."

"How did things go when you arrived at the farm?" asked Cst. Herman.

"Nancy blew up. I don't even know why. I don't think anybody knew why. I don't think *she* knew why. Her mom and dad got really upset and told us to leave the property. Before we could leave, the local police showed up and escorted us away. There were no charges. I don't know what happened after that. Ernie and I just drove back to Chicago; minus Nancy, and minus the cocaine."

"What happened the next time you came to the farm?" asked Cst. Herman.

"We never went to that farm again. I don't know what you're talking about," said Johnnie. He was getting quite loud, but he stayed in his seat. "Did someone say we went back to the farm?"

Chief O'Donnell stuck his head in the door and said, "Is everything okay in here?"

Johnnie settled down and said, "Talk to Ernie. Talk to anybody. We've never been anywhere close to that farm, since. Heck, we've only been in Canada a couple of times until this latest trip to Hamilton."

"Oh, we'll check all right," said Chief Petrovic. "Where were you on October 3, 1911?"

"I don't know for certain," said Johnnie. "That was a long time ago. I know that Ernie and I got busted for something about that time. It might've been for violating parole. It wasn't a big deal, but they locked us up for thirty days in the Chicago jail. It was around that time you're asking about, but I don't know for sure. I guess you'll have to check with the Chicago police. They probably have a record of it. They've always been concerned about my welfare," he said with a smirk. "They think I should be safe inside."

"You can be certain we'll check that out with the police in Chicago," said Chief Petrovic. "Until we do have it checked out, you're to stay in the immediate vicinity of Hamilton at a location where we can find you. You are excused for now."

Johnnie got up and left.

"Just stay here in the interview room and keep an eye out for Ernie Stanzio, in case he appears before I get back," said Chief Petrovic to Cst. Herman. "I'm going to go and find Chief O'Donnell and ask him to arrange a surety bond with Beno Stanzio for Johnnie and Ernie to ensure they remain in the area until I've heard back from Chicago about their alibi."

Chief Petrovic was back in five minutes. Within a minute or so of returning, there was a rap on the door. Cst. Herman opened the door and then introduced himself and Chief Petrovic to Ernie Stanzio. They interviewed Ernie using almost identical questions to the ones they had used with Johnnie Polizzi and the answers they got from Ernie were almost identical to the answers they'd received from Johnnie.

Ernie was excused with the same admonishment to stay in the area.

As soon as they were by themselves, Chief Petrovic turned to Cst. Herman and said, "What did you make of the interviews?"

"I'm disappointed, Chief," said Cst. Herman. "We didn't get a confession, and I don't think these guys cooked the story up ahead of time. I don't know what to think. Everything else seems to fit them to the crime. Both Polizzi and Stanzio were identified in the police report as being present at the big dustup at the Featherstone farm, we have the neighbors as witnesses, and this all happened just a couple week before the fatal fire. I guess the next thing we do is just wait and see what the police in Chicago have to say."

"They didn't seem overly alarmed about being interviewed," said the chief. "It's as if they really don't know anything about the fire at the Featherstone farm. We didn't tell them about it either."

Then a thought suddenly seemed to occur to Chief Petrovic. Cst. Herman saw the expression on the chief's face change and the chief jumped up.

"Excuse me, Peter, but I need to get a hold of Johnnie or Ernie before they get out of the building."

Five minutes later, Chief Petrovic was back in the interview room with Chief O'Donnell and Johnnie Polizzi. Chief O'Donnell excused himself.

"What's going on?" said Johnnie. "I thought we were done? I answered all the questions as best I could."

"I believe you," said Chief Petrovic. "Thank you for coming back. I have one more question that I forgot to ask you. When was the last time you saw Nancy Featherstone?"

"I'm not sure," said Johnnie. "I don't think she went back to De-Paul. The next time I saw her, she was hanging with a slightly different crowd. All her friends seemed to have money. She was too good for me and Ernie. We saw her maybe two or three times over the next year. I remember Ernie and I bumped into her in downtown Chicago, just after New Year's, in 1912. I may have seen her occasionally since then, but she's never acknowledged me, so I'm not one hundred percent certain it was her. You know how sometimes you see somebody and they look like somebody you know, then when you go to speak to them you realize they're not who you thought they were?"

"Yes. Thanks, Johnnie. That's really helpful," said Chief Petrovic. "I won't drag you back in again today."

Johnnie Polizzi left and Cst. Herman sat there with a puzzled expression on his face.

"How did you ever think of asking that question?" he said to the chief.

"I just played a hunch. I'm as surprised as you are by the answer Johnnie gave us. Earlier, when we had completed the interviews and we were discussing what we either had or had not found out, you said 'everything else seems to fit them to the crime'. The words 'fit them' bothered me. We were trying to fit them, but maybe they didn't fit. Maybe we were making the crime simpler than it really was."

"Knowing Nancy Featherstone might still be alive shakes up any theory I had," said Cst. Herman.

"And it poses another huge question," said Chief Petrovic. "Whose body was found in the fire? It has always been assumed that it was Nancy Featherstone."

"We're done in Hamilton. Let's get some supper and then head back to Chaseford."

GEORGIE AND I WERE sitting on the only two half-comfortable chairs in my bachelor flat at the back of Franklin's Groceries.

"What time did you tell them to be here, Joel?" asked Georgie.

"Somewhere around 7:30," I said.

Earlier, Georgie had reminded me that today was March 3rd.

"In less than three months you'll have a new boss," said Georgie.

"I don't know what you're talking about," I said.

I saw storm clouds gathering, and for a moment I thought Georgie was going to lose it and demonstrate the authoritarian side of her nature.

"Oh, are you referring to our wedding on the first of June?" I said.

My quick recovery avoided a tiff that would've happened just as our company arrived. Either that or I was saved by the bell.

Jay and Sylvia are our best friends and we were looking forward to a pleasant evening. Neither Jay nor I knew how Chief Petrovic's trip to Hamilton had went. He and Cst. Herman were not due back until sometime this evening.

The four of us spent a few minutes speculating about the Hamilton expedition. Were they going to bring a suspect back? Jay and I talked too much at home and as a result Sylvia and Georgie knew more than they should about police business. Fortunately, they also knew how to keep a secret.

We played euchre for a while, the girls against the guys. Once again, the girls trounced us mercilessly. We stopped and had one of my favourite winter treats: hot chocolate and popcorn balls. As we were finishing off our snack, Georgie suggested we try a guessing game.

"I guess so," said Jay.

Jay's quip gave us all a good laugh. About every five minutes, for the rest of the night, someone would say 'I guess so' and everyone would laugh again.

We did the same guessing game with the cards that Georgie and I had played with Gwen Cummings. Each of us had three turns to guess three cards correctly. That meant each of us had nine opportunities to guess the hidden card.

After one round, no one had made a single correct guess. We were 0 for 9, or a big fat 0%. Certainly, no telepathy was showing up here. We persevered through three rounds. Out of the 36 guesses, we only had one correct guess. Jay had gotten lucky when he'd guessed the first card on his second set of three.

"That game is no fun," said Sylvia. "Cross that game off your entertainment list."

"I guess so," said Georgie.

We all laughed and then played some more euchre. The girls were still too good for us. Our pleasant evening ended, and Jay and Sylvia returned to Baby Brad.

After they left, Georgie said, "Did you record the numbers you really thought you sensed?"

"I did. I jotted them down on this piece of paper," I said.

While we were playing, I had reported a number that was different from the number I had actually sensed. Georgie and I had planned this ahead of time. For everyone else's benefit, I was to report any playing card other than the one that I actually sensed. Then I would record the value of the playing card I had really sensed on a piece of paper. Jay and Sylvia had probably just assumed I was recording the numbers that I had spoken aloud.

I handed the page that listed the cards I had sensed to Georgie. She compared the list to the list of actual cards exposed during my turns.

"I don't believe it," she said. "Your real score was eight out of nine."

Monday, March 6th

THERE WAS ALWAYS SOMEONE to be brought up to date on something. The chief felt the 9 o'clock Monday morning meetings in his office were important to keep his constables together as a team. When everyone knew what was going on, it provided an excellent environment for the exploration of ideas relevant to the investigation. More ideas, more leads, more clues, more likely to solve the case was the way Chief Petrovic thought.

Chief Petrovic summed up the interviews he and Cst. Herman had conducted in Hamilton for the other three constables. When he reached the point in his summary where he called Johnnie Polizzi back for the final question he paused. There were some quizzical looks. When he continued, and talked about the final question and Polizzi's response, the quizzical looks turned to near astonishment.

Cst. Herman looked at his fellow constables and chuckled. "I was as astonished as you are," he said.

"It leaves us with two key questions," said Chief Petrovic. "Whose remains were found when the Featherstone house burned down in 1911? And where is Nancy Featherstone? What suggestions do you have that would lead us to the answers to those questions?"

"We're going to have to try to locate any neighbours, friends, or relatives of the Featherstones that are still alive," said Cst. Smith. "Then we're going to have to question them about any relatives or people that may have visited them or worked for them in the fall of 1911."

"Good idea, Cst. Smith," said the chief. "With Cst. Jarvis's help, you can start on that process once the meeting is over. Take a look at the reports from the fire investigation and also talk to Henry Featherstone. Remember, he's the nephew of the deceased couple and the current owner of the farm. He might be the best source of information.

"Any other ideas?" asked the chief.

"Sir, I suggest we contact the Chicago Police Department to see if they have any incident reports from 1911 or 1912 that mention a woman named Nancy Featherstone," I said. "Perhaps we could also get them to check Chicago and area directories for her name."

"Good idea, Cst. Franklin," said the chief.

"Peter, with Joel's help, I want you to get started on that. I also want you to check to see if anybody with that name lives in Canada. You may have to contact the Census Canada headquarters. There's an office in Toronto.

"If there are no further suggestions or questions the meeting is over. I want you to get on these tasks as soon as you can; at the same time, I don't want them to interfere with your other daily police duties." Chief Petrovic dismissed the constables.

CST. SMITH WON THE coin flip with Cst. Jay Jarvis. Cst. Smith used his choice to line up an interview with Henry Featherstone. He felt that, if anybody had information that would be helpful, it would be Henry, the nephew of the deceased owners.

Cst. Jay Jarvis on the other hand was to start interviewing the neighbours. The person with the most information was likely to be Jenny Kaufman. Mrs. Kaufman was 87 years old. She was almost blind and could only hear what she wanted to. But her mind was still good. Especially for things that happened years ago. She lived with one of her granddaughters in Chaseford. In 1911, and for several years prior to that, she and her husband had lived on the farm next to the Featherstones' place. She had always been a very inquisitive person.

CONSTABLE JAKE SMITH told Henry Featherstone they were after some background information.

"With the discoveries in the icehouse at the farm, we're starting an investigation into the possible murders of your aunt and uncle."

"Finding the bodies in the icehouse at the farm after all this time was quite a surprise," said Henry. "My father was very hurt when they disappeared so suddenly without letting him know and without ever contacting him. My dad and his brother were good friends. He often wondered if something bad hadn't happened to them. I'll help you as much as I can." Henry paused for a moment, reflecting, and then added, "You know, Nancy's body was found in the ashes of the house during the fire investigation back in 1911. It now seems likely that all three of them were murdered at the same time. This has become an even more terrible tragedy."

Cst. Smith didn't know what to say. It wasn't his place to share the police chief's theory about Nancy Featherstone, especially at this point in time. But he did need to get as much information as he could about the people and events at the Featherstone farm in 1911. At that time, everyone assumed it was Nancy Featherstone's body that had been found. It may have been. But in a murder investigation they had to consider all possibilities.

"I know it's a long time ago," said Cst. Smith, "but I need you to try and recall if there were any other people that visited the Featherstone farm regularly in 1911."

"No, I can't think of anyone," Henry Featherstone responded, "but that was a long time ago."

"Were there any young women or men that worked on the farm or worked in the house helping your aunt? It was a large house."

"Yes, I remember now," said Henry. "There was a girl that the Featherstones brought to the farm when she was about 10 years old. She was maybe four years younger than me. We spoke occasionally, whenever I visited my uncle's farm, and she seemed like a nice person.

"There's quite a story to this, actually. My aunt was a generous person who liked other people. She could usually see beyond people's faults. My aunt and uncle were very well off and my aunt always felt it was important to share your good fortune with those less fortunate. She had contacted the Salvation Army in England and had arranged to have a girl brought over to Canada. I don't think she was ever legally adopted, but they treated her like a daughter. She helped out on the farm until probably 1909 or 1910 and then, with the Featherstones' blessing and some financial help, she moved to Toronto, where she got a job in a clothing factory. She would come back at least once a year for a visit. She got along well with my aunt and uncle."

"Did she get along with Nancy?" asked Cst. Smith.

"I don't know," said Henry. "Nancy didn't seem to have much to do with her. After grade eight, Nancy didn't have much to do with anyone in the area. Nancy was about the same age as me. She didn't go to the local high school. Her parents sent her away to an expensive private school. I'm not sure whether it was in Toronto or somewhere in the states; maybe Chicago. She was also away quite often in the summer for several weeks, at exclusive camps. She was rarely at home at all when she was a teenager. Occasionally, she would have girlfriends here from the private school she attended."

"What was the name of the girl that the Featherstones brought over from England?" asked Cst. Smith.

"I was never formally introduced to her. I just called her Sue and she didn't seem to object," Henry answered.

"If you come across her name, or talk to someone who remembers her name, please let me know," said Cst. Smith, ending the interview.

CONSTABLE JAY JARVIS couldn't interview old Jenny Kaufman until 3 o'clock. Jenny's granddaughter had a medical appointment and wouldn't be back home until three.

When Jay arrived at the house, punctually at three, Jenny's grand-daughter Adeline introduced him to Jenny twice. Jenny's hearing difficulties were the source of the confusion in the first introduction. With her ear trumpet in place things improved. She was disappointed he was not a grandson she had not met before because he seemed like a fine young man, but she was somewhat mollified when she understood he was a police constable. This meant she must be important to some investigation.

"I understand you are quite well-informed about things, Mrs. Kaufman," said Cst. Jay Jarvis.

"Oh yes, I have a great memory for things that happened a while ago, and when I was younger I had keen investigative skills. I was never involved with the police, but I tried to accumulate as much information about people as I possibly could. That way, if they got into difficulty because they couldn't remember something, I could tell them what it was they forgot. I was also quite interested in human relationships. It's important to know who is a friend to whom."

Cst. Jarvis could see this might go on for some time, so he tried to interrupt gracefully. In a brief pause between words, he quickly interjected, "We've heard of your prodigious memory, Mrs. Kaufmann."

At these words the old lady smiled and fell silent.

"The question I'm going to ask you," said Jay, "has to do with the time you spent on the farm."

"Oh yes," she said. "That's when my inquisitive skills were at their peak."

Before she could get started again Jay said, "It's about the Featherstone farm." He spoke quickly, to avoid being interrupted himself. "It's been a lot of years since the fire, but with the discovery of body parts in the icehouse the police have opened a murder investigation. We're now trying to collect as much information as we possibly can about events that may have happened on the farm in the fall of 1911."

The old woman brightened considerably. "Yes! Yes! Yes!" she said. "Ask me anything!" And to Jay's surprise she became quiet, leaned toward him with her ear trumpet in place, and waited for the question.

"The body of a young woman was found in the ashes of the fire," said Cst. Jarvis.

"Oh yes, poor Nancy Featherstone," said Mrs. Kaufman interrupting the constable. "That was a tragedy."

Cst. Jarvis knew enough not to correct Mrs. Kaufman, even if he'd been at liberty to. "I want you to test your memory," he said. "In 1911, or before, were there any other people that worked on the farm or that helped in the house at the Featherstone property?"

Mrs. Kaufman was literally beaming. "Of course," she said. "The Featherstones brought that young girl over from England. She was a nice girl. I think she was only about 10 years old when she came over. I would see her occasionally, but she was a very poor source of information. She would just bid me a good day, smile, and go on her way. I wasn't sure whether she was a little bit – how do you say it? – slow, or whether she had been told not to speak to strangers. Especially me. But what would you like to know about the girl?"

"Do you recall her name?" asked Jay.

"Her name was an earful," said Mrs. Kaufman. "Henrietta Harriet Hackelby was her given name. I got that much out of her, at least. The Featherstones called her Henny." Mrs. Kaufman added, "But that girl left the farm for Toronto in mid-October 1910. Let me think. It was October 16, the same day my granddaughter Melody was born. I knew I could remember."

Jay waited patiently.

"Henny was good about coming back to visit with the Featherstones. She was back the end of June 1911. But I don't remember seeing her again after that."

Cst. Jay Jarvis realized he'd been with the old woman for almost an hour. It had seemed considerably longer, but he had received some valuable information. It was time to leave.

"Mrs. Kaufman, it was my pleasure to meet you," said Jay. "You've been a great help to me. You're a storehouse of information."

The old woman had started to smile and couldn't stop. It was clear that this young Cst. Jay Jarvis was the best policeman she'd ever met. She asked him to stay for tea.

"I'm honoured by the invitation," said Jay. "Unfortunately, I have other police duties I promised the chief I would attend to."

Reluctantly, Mrs. Kaufman let him go.

IT WAS ABOUT 3:30 MONDAY afternoon when Cst. Smith came back to the police station to report his findings to Chief Petrovic. He told the chief that the only interview he had conducted that afternoon was with Henry Featherstone.

"I think I found out something important from Henry Featherstone this afternoon," said Cst. Smith. "Henry told me about a girl that had been brought over from England to help the Featherstones on the farm. She helped them on the farm until sometime in 1909 or 1910. By the time she left the farm she was likely close to twenty years old. I'm sorry, but Henry couldn't remember her name. He doesn't think he was ever told."

About half an hour later, Cst. Jay Jarvis arrived at the police station. He walked into the chief's office, looked at Cst. Smith and said, "I think you rigged the coin flip. Do you have a two-headed coin?"

"Oh, you're back from your interview with Mrs. Kaufman, are you? Did you get a word in edgewise?" asked Cst. Smith with a look of mock concern.

Cst. Smith and Chief Petrovic laughed.

"The good news is, I got some interesting information, Chief. Did you know that the Featherstones brought a girl over from England around the turn-of-the-century?"

"I do know that," replied the chief. "Cst. Smith gave me that information half an hour ago. Were you able to find out her last name?"

"According to the local encyclopedia of events, past and current, Jenny Kaufman, the girl's name was Henrietta Harriet Hackelby," replied Cst. Jarvis.

"Congratulations constables. You did a good job this afternoon," said the chief. "This information could prove valuable. First thing tomorrow morning I'll talk to constables Herman and Franklin. They need to add the name Henrietta Harriet Hackelby to their search list."

Friday, March 10th

THE CHIEF CALLED A special meeting for Friday afternoon, at 1:30 PM, in his office. He wanted to summarize what they had discovered so far in their investigations surrounding the disappearance of Nancy Featherstone and the murder of her parents.

Chief Petrovic started the meeting by recounting the success achieved at the start of the week by Cst. Herbert and Cst. Jarvis. Through their interviews, they had determined that a young woman, Henrietta Harriet Hackelby, had lived on the Featherstone farm until about the age of twenty.

"I passed this name on to Cst. Herman and Cst. Franklin," said the chief. "They were to contact the Census office in Toronto to attempt to trace her whereabouts, as well as the whereabouts of Nancy Featherstone. Cst. Herman will now report on their findings to date."

"We haven't had any success," said Cst. Herman. "The latest Canadian Census of 1931 did not include either name, and our contact with the Chicago Police Department did not provide us with any new information. There was no mention of a Nancy Featherstone in any incident report in Chicago from 1911 or 1912. They don't have Nancy Featherstone's name on file anywhere. Her name has also not appeared in any of the Chicago and area directories. The same turned out to be true for the name Henrietta Harriet Hackelby."

Chief Petrovic said, "We have to track down all possible leads. I know it can be frustrating, but if you get to the end of a blind alley, at least you know you have to consider other possibilities. Cst. Herman and Cst. Franklin have not been able to locate either name to date. What are the other possibilities that this suggests?"

"I suppose they could either be dead or they could have changed their names," said Cst. Jarvis.

"Very good, Jay," said the chief. "What would be our next move?"

"We would have to check death certificates and marriage certificates, or change of name forms," said Jay.

"To start with, we will check the records for Ontario and the Chicago area only," said Chief Petrovic. "I want the four of you to get together on your own after this meeting to decide who will search what records. You will have to determine where the records are located. Then you will have to contact those locations by telephone. You're to start on those searches on Monday morning."

Chief Petrovic continued, "The Chicago Police Department got back to me late yesterday with regard to the whereabouts of Johnnie Polizzi and Ernie Stanzio on October 3, 1911. They were in a jail cell in Chicago for the entire month of October that year for violating parole. As far as I'm concerned, that clears them from any direct involvement in the fire or the murder of the Featherstones."

AS A FRIDAY NIGHT TREAT, Georgie and I went to the movies. The main feature was a crime mystery, *The Thin Man*, starring William Powell and Myrna Loy. Georgie teased me about my choice of film. She said "You can't give up police work even for Friday night. There are a couple of differences, though: you are not a detective yet, and I am not your wealthy wife."

After the show, we went back to my place. There wasn't much room, but we had our privacy. We got talking about the case and how we were having trouble locating the two women.

"What does Walter think?" said Georgie.

"I don't know. I haven't communicated with him lately. I've been busy, and I guess I have been thinking too much about you," I said with a wink.

"Oh, you are such a sweet talker," she replied with a better wink than mine. "I think it's getting warm in here. But first things first: contact Walter."

I thought, "Walter", and I was in immediate contact with him. I started to apologize about not talking to him lately. Walter interrupted.

"Joel, time is not the same for me as it is for you. Are you any older than you were when we first met in 1928? Of course you are. Am I any older? Of course not. I'm not alive. You're living and time is going by. Everything around you is changing. Even the house at 200 Durham Street is getting older, though much more slowly than you are. I just am."

I had a sudden thought. "So, everything that happened while you were alive is in order like a movie, but once your life has ended it's like time is suspended and all that had happened seems like it just happened? Is that how it works?"

As I communicated with Walter, I repeated everything out loud to Georgie so that she could follow my train of thought.

"That's probably the best way to explain it to a person who is alive," replied Walter.

"So you and Louise Carter and Floyd, the essence that Gwen Cummings has contact with, experience things much the same way?"

"Certainly," answered Walter.

"I'm working on a case," I started.

Walter interrupted me. "You're talking about the body parts case. I wondered why you never got back to me about that. In an earlier conversation, I told you that local essences were not aware of anyone being dismembered. That could be because the victims were dead long before it happened. They were never in it state of extreme fear or anger because they were *anticipating* an impending dismemberment. Do you know any more about the case now?"

"I have a location," I replied. "Our investigations have led us to believe that the Featherstones were dismembered at their farm, and that another person, a young woman, was murdered there as well. Her body was found in the fire that happened in October 1911."

I don't know whether an essence can get excited, but I thought I sensed agitation from Walter. I received a thought from him about a presence at the Featherstone farm.

"There is someone like me at the Featherstone farm," said Walter. "She rarely sends out a message. I don't even know her name. I sensed that she was disturbed recently. I can't tell by calendar time, but I can tell by order of communications that her disturbance happened between the last time you talked to me and now."

"I'm going out to the farm to see if I can contact her," I said. "If she is who I think she is, I know some things that may trigger a connection. For example, her name, and possibly who murdered her. Walter, please try to contact her as soon as you can to let her know I'm coming out to the farm. Let me know if you receive a message."

I stopped communicating with Walter and looked at Georgie. "That was quite a session," said Georgie.

"I'm very glad you suggested contacting Walter," I replied. "I think I need to visit the farm to try and meet the essence there. I suspect it's Henrietta Harriet Hackelby."

"Tomorrow is Saturday," said Georgie. "Let's go in the afternoon."

I thought that was a good suggestion.

Saturday, March 11th

I DROPPED INTO FRANKLIN'S Groceries around 9 o'clock Saturday morning. I didn't have far to go, since I lived at the back of the store, behind the wall of stacked supply boxes.

"Dad, I was wondering if I could borrow the car this afternoon to take Georgie for a ride in the country."

"That's not a problem, Joel," said Mr. Franklin. "You don't ask for the car much. I'm glad to lend it to you. Georgie's a wonderful girl. She'll be a fine boss." He grinned. "It's supposed to be a beautiful day in any case, so I'll enjoy the ten-minute walk home. I'm leaving the store around 3 o'clock this afternoon. Your brother Ralph can handle things until closing time."

My dad hadn't said much about it, but I know he was still not certain what he and mom were going to do if Ralph's tryout with the Cleveland Indians was successful and he ended up leaving Chaseford to play minor league ball in the summer. The family budget was fairly tight, and I knew my dad wasn't sure whether they could afford to hire any paid part-time help for the store.

IT WAS A BEAUTIFUL late-winter Saturday afternoon. I drove to Georgie's house in my dad's 1928 Model A Ford sedan and picked her up about 1:30 PM for the trip to the farm. I had called Henry Featherstone earlier in the morning to get his permission to wander around the burned-out remains of the old house on what had at one time been his uncle's farm. He knew I was a police constable, so he wasn't surprised by the request. He just assumed I was doing some more sleuthing.

When we arrived at the farm gate we had a pleasant surprise: the lane to the house was in drivable condition. The last time I had been to the farm, a couple of weeks previously, there'd still been a lot of snow on the lane. We'd had a few days of above-average temperature before it cooled down again this past Wednesday, so a lot of the snow had gone.

Georgie and I got out of the car and walked over to the remains of what had once been a very large home. Each of us carried a good-size walking stick so we could test the floor ahead of us while we wandered around what was left of the ground floor of the building.

"I wish I knew were the body had been found," I said to Georgie. "That location would probably be optimal for attempting to contact Harriet, or Henny, as most people knew her."

We used our heavy sticks to tap our way to roughly the middle of the main floor of the original structure. It was difficult to tell, exactly, because part of the second story had collapsed onto the first. We had to be very careful as we made our way around the charred chunks of the former home.

I stopped and indicated to Georgie that I was going to attempt to communicate. During my attempt to communicate, I would not be speaking, but concentrating, and Georgie would not likely hear or see anything unusual. I said I would not speak aloud to her until my communications with Henny were completed. I needed to focus all my efforts on contacting Henny.

I FOCUSED ON HENNY by sending, "Henrietta, can you hear me? Henrietta? Can you hear me?"

I sensed nothing.

"I have a special ability that allows me to communicate with troubled spirits, Henny. My friend Walter told me he would try to contact you. He's not alive either. He had a terrible death too."

Now I had the first feeling that something – or rather, *someone* – was nearby.

"I know someone killed you," I continued. "I think you were murdered by Nancy Featherstone."

I thought I sensed "yes".

"Your full name is Henrietta Harriet Hackelby," I said.

Then I sensed something unusual: laughter. It was so clear that I looked at Georgie to see if she could hear it too. Evidently not.

"That's not my name," came across to me exceptionally clearly. "My name is, or was, Henrietta Harriet Allenby."

This revelation explained why our record searches had not been successful. I guess Jenny Kaufman's memory was not as perfect as she thought it was. We had made a poor assumption: we had assumed that an older woman's memory had given us a name that we could treat as a fact. A lesson to be learned.

I communicated with Henny for several more minutes. Obviously, any information I could get might be helpful in solving the murders, but I would have to be careful about how I shared the information with my fellow officers. I couldn't say, "Henrietta Harriet Allenby told me. Yes, the girl who was murdered more than twenty years ago." If I talked that way, the authorities might decide I'd earned a vacation in a padded room.

Henny communicated to me in detail what had happened the day of the murders. She had arrived from Toronto the evening before to visit the Featherstones. She'd managed to save a little money from her job in Toronto; enough to buy a used Model T Ford. She was proud of her purchase and had wanted to show it off to the Featherstones. When Henny arrived, she immediately noticed Nancy's different behaviour. Henny told me that she recalled most of the conversation she'd had with Nancy when they were by themselves that evening.

It went as follows:

"Are you feeling okay, Nancy?" Henny had asked.

"I feel terrific, as long as I have a good snort of cocaine." Nancy had giggled and said, "You can't say anything about the cocaine to my mom and dad. They'd just get extremely upset. How about you, Henny? Do you want some to snort?"

"No thanks, I'm not into that," Henny had replied.

"Good, because I'm running out, and when I run out, I'll be the meanest person you've ever met," Nancy had said. "You don't want to be around here when my supply is gone."

Nancy had then made a lot of derogatory comments about her parents. She'd said she would get even with them. Her remarks had made no sense to Henny. She'd suspected Nancy was suffering from paranoia because she had consumed so much cocaine.

Nancy's parents appeared to have been concerned for her, and for that reason had not let her return to DePaul University in Chicago, where they thought she had been introduced to the drug. It had seemed to Henny that they were trying to help her.

At breakfast on the morning of October 3rd, the day of the fire, Mr. and Mrs. Featherstone had told Nancy that they had made arrangements for her to go to a sanatorium in the Muskoka district. Upon hearing this, Nancy had looked wildly at all of them and exclaimed they were "evil". She'd jumped up from the table and raced from the room, shouting, "You will all be punished!"

"Nancy seemed to have settled down by lunch time," Henny continued, "but she still had a strange look on her face. The Featherstones often had wine with their lunch. Prior to lunch, Nancy proposed a toast to the future. This was a strange gesture from Nancy, but we decided to humour her. That was our mistake. The wine was poisoned. Mr. and Mrs. Featherstone both died within minutes. I'd only taken a tiny amount of the poisoned wine, but it was enough to incapacitate me and leave me in a semiconscious state.

"I watched as Nancy dragged the bodies of her parents out through the rear door of the home into the nearby workshop. She then returned for me. She bound me securely and gagged me and informed me that I would burn in hell. She then told me she was sorry her parents had died because she wanted to torture them because they were evil. She told me I would have a hot death and her parents would have a cold death. She left me bound and gagged on the dining room floor for a couple of hours. When she returned to the room, she had my suitcase and my car keys. She then told me she was going to set the house on fire and that she hoped it would take a long time to burn and that I would suffer a lot. She was crazy."

WHEN HENNY FINISHED, I just sat there. I must have sat very still for more than a minute because Georgie came over and shook my shoulder.

"Are you okay, Joel?" she asked.

"I'm fine. I'm just overwhelmed by the story that Henny told me." I repeated to Georgie as much of Henny's communication as I could remember. I think Georgie was just about as stunned as I was by what had been revealed.

Henny had given me more information than I had ever anticipated. Unfortunately, this information was in the form of a conversation with someone that no longer existed. I would have to plan carefully how to use it. The one piece of information that I needed to use right away was Henny's last name. The police couldn't go on searching for someone with the name Hackelby. It would be a waste of time.

Georgie and I talked about this.

"I think the best approach would be to suggest to Chief Petrovic that it could be worthwhile checking the British Home Children immigration records to verify the name of the child that the Featherstones brought to Canada," said Georgie. "But I think you should wait until your Monday meeting. No one's life hangs in the balance. If you were to suddenly call Chief Petrovic on the weekend, he would wonder why you thought it so urgent."

I agreed with her.

"I'm getting cold and I'm getting hungry," said Georgie. "If we head back to town now, we've got time to go to Mabel's Diner for a cup of hot chocolate and one of her special pastries."

"Now you're reading *my* mind," I said.

"That's a very easy task, Joel," said Georgie.

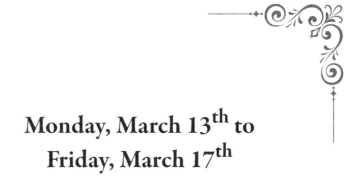

Monday, March 13th to
Friday, March 17th

THERE WAS NO REGULAR Monday morning meeting this week, so when I dropped in to see the chief just after 9 o'clock Monday morning he looked up at me and said, "Joel, there's no meeting this morning. We had the meeting Friday afternoon."

"I know, Chief, but I had a thought on the weekend."

"I like a dedicated constable," said the chief. "What was your thought?"

"I know Jenny Kaufman has a reputation for being an authority on everyone's business, but she is an older woman and nobody's memory is perfect. We've been hunting through records for the names Henrietta Harriet Hackelby and Nancy Featherstone without success. We know Nancy Featherstone's name is accurate, and her name hasn't come up in our search; which implies either that she's dead, or she's not using that name. But we don't know for certain that Henrietta Harriet Hackelby is the name of the girl that the Featherstones brought over from England.

"I think we should be checking immigration records, or perhaps even records from the British Salvation Army, from about 1898 to 1903, searching under the name Featherstone. If we locate their name, then we will have the name of the child they took into care. That will verify whether it was Henrietta Harriet Hackelby or not."

"That's a long speech, Joel, but it is a very good idea. I want you to check with the Department of Immigration. Let me know what you come up with as soon as possible. We will put a temporary hold on our other searches until we can verify the name of the girl that the Featherstones brought to Canada."

IT WAS A LITTLE AFTER 3 o'clock Tuesday afternoon when Chief Petrovic called me to his telephone. "I think you should take this call, Joel," he said.

It was a woman calling from the Department of Immigration records office.

"Is that Cst. Joel Franklin?" she asked.

"This is Cst. Franklin," I replied.

"I'm looking at a record dated May 15, 1901," she said. "It says that an 11-year-old girl named Henrietta Harriet Allenby was taken into care on this date by Harold Featherstone and Marion Featherstone of RR 3 Chaseford, in the province of Ontario."

"That's great," I shouted into the telephone. Then, in a quieter tone, "I'm very sorry. I didn't mean to be so loud. I'm just excited."

That phone call changed the direction of our inquiry.

CST. PETER HERMAN CONTACTED the Chicago police again. This time he told them the name he was looking for was Henrietta Harriet Allenby. He asked the Chicago police if they could check their incident books from 1911 and 1912 for any mention of her name. He suggested that, if there was an incident, it was likely drug-related. Next, Cst. Herman contacted the Illinois Bell telephone company and inquired if they had any listings for anyone with the last name of Allenby in their directories for Chicago and area from 1911 to 1914. Both the police department and Illinois Bell told Cst. Herman they would get back to him within a day or two.

Meanwhile, Cst. Jay Jarvis had contacted the Bureau of Statistics office in Toronto. He inquired if they would do a search for the name Henrietta Harriet Allenby in the Census data from 1911, 1921, and 1931. They replied that they would try to contact him within a week.

CST. HERMAN RECEIVED a call early Friday from the Illinois Bell telephone company. He was informed that there had been a listing for a Harriet Allenby living in Chicago in 1913. There was no listing in 1914. The person from Bell returning Cst. Herman's call had also checked the directories of 1915 and 1916 without success.

Monday, March 20th

CHIEF PETROVIC HUNG up the telephone and called the meeting to order.

He turned to his group of constables and said, "That was a call from the Canadian census bureau office in Toronto. They've completed their search for 1916 and 1921 and have found no trace of anyone called Henrietta Harriet Allenby. I told them how much we appreciated their efforts and said we no longer required them to search through the census information for 1926 and 1931.

"I think everyone present is aware that the Illinois Bell telephone company informed us that they had a telephone listing for a Harriet Allenby in their 1913 directory for Rockford, Illinois, but nothing since that time. If our hypothesis is correct, that means that Nancy Featherstone assumed Miss Allenby's identity and travelled, most likely to Chicago, in October 1911. After she had murdered her parents and Henrietta Harriet Allenby.

"Since we have no record of her after that, I think we can further assume that she changed her last name; most likely by marriage. And that she has become a citizen of the United States of America."

"How easy is it to become an American citizen?" asked Cst. Smith.

"The short answer to your question, Cst. Smith, is that the process described under the United States naturalization laws of 1907 can be completed in about five years," said Chief Petrovic.

"That means she could've been an American citizen as early as 1916," said Cst. Herbert.

"So, if we charged her with the crime, I guess we would have to go through the extradition process," I said.

"That's right, Joel," said Chief Petrovic.

"What crime would we charge her with?" asked Cst. Jarvis.

That question got all of us talking at once.

"Quiet," snapped Chief Petrovic. "Let's hear your thoughts. One at a time, starting with Cst. Smith."

"Well, Chief, my first thoughts were murder, arson, car theft, and theft of personal items."

"After that list, Cst. Smith, I don't think anybody else needs a turn," said the chief. "Let's hear your comments."

"It's been over twenty years since the car went missing," said Cst. Herman. "Nobody reported it stolen. We have no idea where it is. It could be a pile of scrap metal. I don't think it's a supportable charge."

"It's difficult to prove murder charges when you don't have the bodies," I said. "We think it was Henny Allenby's body that was discovered more than twenty years ago in the burned-out remains of the Featherstone home, but we can't tell for certain. We suspect that the body parts that have been discovered belong to Harold and Marion Featherstone, Nancy Featherstone's parents, but they've been frozen so long in the icehouse that even the forensic laboratory in Toronto can't accurately confirm their identity. So, we really don't have the bodies of the murder victims as far as the court is concerned."

"That's an excellent analysis, Joel," said Chief Petrovic. "That's the problem with our entire case. As strongly as we feel that terrible things have been done and that they need to be redressed, we need proof. Supposition is not good enough. Coincidence is not good enough. Do some more thinking right now. Where do we go from here?"

"The murders happened so long ago that I don't think we're going to find any direct evidence," said Cst. Herman. "There are no living witnesses. So, if we're lucky, she told somebody. The only people I can think of that she would've told are Johnnie Polizzi and Ernie Stanzio."

"We need to find something that shows they were in contact with one another after October 1911. The most likely source for that would be an arrest or public disturbance report," said Cst. Jarvis.

"I have an idea," said Chief Petrovic. "We did consult with the Chicago police force and they found no incident reports involving the three of them in 1911 or 1912. But thinking back to what was said earlier in this morning's meeting, we need to contact the police in Rockford, Illinois. That's the directory where Harriet Allenby's phone number was listed.

"Cst. Jarvis, I want you to make that contact today. Have them check their incident reports for anything involving Henrietta Harriet Allenby."

Wednesday, March 22nd
to Friday, March 24th

CST. JAY JARVIS WALKED into Chief Petrovic's office at about 11 o'clock on Wednesday morning.

"I just got a telephone call from the Rockford, Illinois, police," he said. "They went back through their incident reports from 1911 and 1912. Their reports showed that the Rockford Police arrested Johnnie Polizzi, Ernie Stanzio, and Henny Allenby for disturbing the peace and resisting arrest on St. Patrick's Day, in March of 1912.

"St. Patrick's Day was on a Sunday that year. The disturbance happened at a private party. When two of the neighbours came over to tell them to tone it down, an altercation ensued and the three of them physically attacked the neighbours. Henny had a knife which she threatened to use. The case never went to court. Charges were dismissed. The neighbours had been drinking too."

"Thank you very much for your hard work, Jay," said Chief Petrovic. "I'm headed to Hamilton as soon as I can make arrangements; most likely tomorrow or Friday at the latest. That information will be useful for my upcoming interview with Johnnie Polizzi and Ernie Stanzio. I'll be taking Cst. Herman with me. He's met Johnnie and Ernie before."

Chief Petrovic immediately got on the phone to Chief O'Donnell in Hamilton. When he was connected to O'Donnell, he said, "Chief Petrovic here. I didn't think we'd be talking again so soon, but something has come up in the investigation I told you about previously and

I need to speak to Ernie Stanzio and Johnnie Polizzi again. They might be able to provide vital information to me in this murder investigation. Please don't let them know how serious the situation is. If you can arrange interviews again through Beno Stanzio that would be very helpful."

"I'm going to a church meeting tonight," said Chief O'Donnell. "That's probably the best place for me to contact Beno without undue concern. I'll keep it low-key. I know that Johnnie and Ernie are currently involved in the purchase of a hardware store in Hamilton. It appears that they want to become Canadian citizens. Hopefully that information helps you."

"Thanks a lot O'Donnell," said Chief Petrovic. "Get back to me as soon as you can with a time for the meeting at the Hamilton police station. I'd really like to have that interview before the end of the week if possible."

CHIEF O'DONNELL CALLED Chief Petrovic back just after lunch on Thursday. The interviews had been arranged to start at 2 o'clock Friday afternoon, at the Hamilton police station. Chief Petrovic had talked to Cst. Herman earlier in the week and told him to be ready to travel to Hamilton either Thursday or Friday.

After an early, but good, lunch at Mabel's Diner, Chief Petrovic and Cst. Herman set off for Hamilton just after 12 noon. Spring was in the air. It was little on the cool side, with a temperature of about 40°F. The highway was basically clear of snow and ice and the sky was blue with the odd fluffy white cloud.

It's a great day for a drive. Especially if you're a passenger, thought Chief Petrovic.

Cst. Herman seemed to be enjoying his chore as the wheelman, too.

They had no trouble finding the Hamilton police station this time. They were even somewhat familiar with the layout of the building by now. They arrived a few minutes early and Chief O'Donnell escorted them to the interview room. He sat and chatted with them for a few minutes.

"Who would you like to see first?" said Chief O'Donnell.

"We'll take the toughest guy first," answered Chief Petrovic. "Send Johnnie Polizzi to us."

WHEN JOHNNIE CAME IN, he was almost friendly. He remembered the last interview as an inconvenience, but it had caused him no harm. He thought they just wanted to check on a couple of details. He sat down and said, "Hello, how can I help you?"

Chief Petrovic had told Cst. Herman he would handle the entire interview. The constable was to take notes and watch facial expressions. Chief Petrovic said they would trade places for the interview with Ernie Stanzio.

"I'll get right to the point, Johnnie," said Chief Petrovic. "You'll recall the last time we were here I asked you about any connection you may have had with Nancy Featherstone."

"That's right," said Johnnie. "I still don't know why you're so interested in Nancy Featherstone."

"That's our business," the chief replied. "You just need to answer our questions and then you're done."

"Fine by me," said Johnnie.

"If you remember," said Chief Petrovic, "I called you back to the interview room for a couple of follow-up questions. I asked you if you had seen Nancy in Chicago in the fall of 1911. You told us yes but that she was hanging with a different crowd. Is that what you said?"

"I think so. You have the notes. I guess that's what I said," answered Johnnie.

"Do you remember St. Patrick's Day in 1912? In Rockford, Illinois?" asked the chief.

Johnnie looked a little confused. His face took on some colour and he hesitantly said, "Sort of."

"I have a police report in front of me, Johnnie. Before I read it to you, I'd like you to tell me what happened. I want to be fair. Give me your side of the story."

"I think there was a misunderstanding after a St. Patrick's Day party. I think we were in Rockford that day," said Johnnie.

"Who was with you that day, Johnnie? I know Ernie was there. I want to know who else was with you and Ernie."

"Ahh, let me think. It was a long time ago," said Johnnie.

"Take your time," said Chief Petrovic. "I have the incident report from the Rockford police in front of me. I know who was there. I'm just testing to see whether you are reliable and responsible in case anybody ever asks me about your character. You know we don't like people who can't be trusted in Canada."

"Okay, 1912, St. Patrick's Day, Rockford, Illinois. I remember now. It was a nice day, so Ernie and I decided to go to Rockford to celebrate St. Patrick's Day with a woman we knew there," said Johnnie.

"You're doing really well, Johnnie. Now just tell me the name of the woman who was at the party with you," snapped Chief Petrovic.

Johnnie Polizzi avoided eye contact with the chief and mumbled, "Nancy Featherstone."

"You forgot to mention that the last time we talked," said the chief.

"Sorry," said Johnnie. "I guess I just didn't remember the incident in Rockfort. I wasn't trying to cause trouble."

"I'll forgive you if you get the answer to the next few questions correct, Johnnie," said the chief. "They're important questions. Especially if you like Canada. If you'd rather return to Chicago and visit with Tony Accardo, that's your choice. The right answers to my questions will likely help you avoid serious charges if you are forthcoming in answering them.

"What name did Nancy give the police in Rockford?"

Johnnie looked really worried. He thought for a moment and then came to a decision. He answered, "She called herself Henny."

"What last name did she use? Speak clearly so I can hear you," said Chief Petrovic.

"She said her name was Henny Allenby."

"Why do you think she used that name, Johnnie?"

"At the time it made no sense to me. I thought she was being difficult with the police, but I didn't say anything then. Later, I found out she had to use that name because it was in the Rockford telephone book."

"The next question is even more difficult," said Chief Petrovic. "But you've been so cooperative, Johnnie, that I hope you answer it truthfully. If you don't, then you're going to face some serious obstruction of justice charges. I know the answer to this question too, Johnnie. What did Nancy Featherstone say happened to her parents?"

Johnnie looked extremely uncomfortable and didn't say anything for almost a minute.

"Remember, I said serious obstruction of justice charges," Chief Petrovic reminded him. "Those charges could potentially lead to more serious charges of aiding and abetting the commission of a serious felony. If you like it in Canada, and have plans, and don't want to spend a long time incarcerated, you'd better give me a truthful answer. Answering me truthfully now will go a long way towards the courts viewing you in a positive light. Answer my question, Johnnie. What did Nancy Featherstone say happened to her parents?"

"We didn't talk about it much," answered Johnnie. "We were all high on cocaine and booze one night in early 1912 when she told Ernie and me that she had killed her parents. She said it happened when she was on coke. She was really stressed and saw them as really evil beings, so she killed them to make the world a better place.

"Did she kill her parents?" Johnnie seemed genuinely surprised. "I don't think I know anybody bad enough that they would kill their own mom and dad, and I know some pretty bad people. That doesn't make any sense. It's against nature."

Chief Petrovic didn't respond.

Johnnie continued, "Ernie and I talked about what she said a little bit, but we didn't take her too seriously. When she was high, she would say anything and do anything. If you got her upset, she could be a dangerous woman. But she could have been making it up, too. We didn't think about it anymore."

"I'm very happy with your cooperation, Johnnie," said Chief Petrovic. "I'm not going to have you detained at this time. Please do not discuss anything we talked about in this interview with anyone else, including Ernie's brother Beno. There is a possibility you could be called as a witness in the future."

"I'm not sure I want to be a witness," said Johnnie.

"I know you'll be a witness," responded the chief. "It's always much better to be a willing witness than to have to be subpoenaed. Thank you, Johnnie, we're done for now."

Johnnie was escorted from the room by a police sergeant and taken directly to the parking lot, where he was instructed to wait for Ernie. Johnnie Polizzi left looking much less content than he'd looked when he'd walked into the interview room.

Cst. Herman and Chief Petrovic talked for a few minutes about what had been revealed in the interview. They were pretty pleased and very excited about the results. The chief said, "Before the interview, I had no idea that Nancy Featherstone would have ever said anything to those two about the death of her parents. Sometimes the good guys get lucky."

Chief Petrovic opened the door of the interview room and asked the police sergeant sitting there to please get Ernie Stanzio and bring him to the interview room.

Now it was Cst. Herman's turn to do the interrogation. He followed Chief Petrovic's pattern from the previous interview question by question. Whenever Cst. Herman encountered any resistance from Ernie, he would inform Ernie that Johnnie had already answered the question successfully. Ernie's interview was much easier than the one the chief had conducted with Johnnie. He offered only minimal resistance.

When asked about Nancy Featherstone, Ernie's answers were almost identical to the ones that Johnnie had given. He was obviously stunned by the implication that what Nancy Featherstone had said might be true. When he was informed that he might be called as a witness, he didn't seem to be concerned. He just wanted the interview to end.

Monday, March 27th

THE 9 O'CLOCK MONDAY morning meeting in the Chaseford Chief of Police's office started with Chief Petrovic announcing that, because of their hard work and the major developments in the murder case at the end of the past week, lunch at Mabel's Diner was on him. It was very noisy for the next couple of minutes.

There was a real air of excitement. They had had a major break in what had started out as 'the body parts case' and that they now viewed as the murder of Harold and Marion Featherstone. They now had two witnesses to Henny Allenby – a.k.a. Nancy Featherstone – confessing to the murder of her parents.

But it wasn't enough to charge Nancy Featherstone with murder. Chief Petrovic was convinced that she had committed the murders, but his opinion wouldn't be enough to satisfy a judge or to support a request for extradition from the United States. Looking at it realistically, his major piece of evidence was a reported conversation Nancy Featherstone had had in Illinois over twenty years ago with two men known to be small-time hoodlums while they were all under the influence of drugs.

Chief Petrovic needed more. He needed a chance to interview Nancy Featherstone. That could be a problem, though, because he had no idea where she was. All searches for the current whereabouts of Nancy Featherstone, now known as Henny Allenby, had arrived at dead ends.

Chief Petrovic called the meeting to order. "We need to do some tough thinking in the next few minutes," he said. "We need an idea. We need to locate Henny Allenby, and we need to get her to Canada."

They discussed the possibility of searching phone directories from across Illinois from the last twenty years, but that idea was quickly dismissed because they were no longer certain of her last name. Finding her last name would mean checking marriage records from all over Illinois and perhaps beyond. That idea was too much like searching for a needle in a haystack. And if they did locate her, that still left the problem of getting her to Canada.

"There was a story in the newspaper the other day about trying to locate someone's next of kin," said Cst. Jay Jarvis. "It was in the Toronto Evening Telegram. The lawyer who'd been appointed executor of the estate had put the story in the paper. It was a sizable estate and two of the people named in the will couldn't be located. They were evidently boyhood chums of the deceased. In the story, the lawyer gave their names and said that if they came forward they would have to provide proof of identification. I think we could do something like that in this case. Although we might have to embellish the truth a bit."

"You mean lie," said Chief Petrovic.

"I don't think we should lie," said Jay, "but perhaps we can choose our words carefully."

"So, if we could create an ad for someone named Henrietta Harriet Allenby that would entice her to lay claim to something that seemed valuable, that would serve the dual purpose of locating her and getting her back to Canada," said Chief Petrovic. "That's a great idea, Jay, but we'll have to be careful what we promise."

"We know that Harold and Marion Featherstone came to a quick and violent demise," I said. "It was a long time ago. Perhaps in their wills they left something to Henny Allenby. If that was the case, then there would be a bequest awaiting her."

"Good idea, Joel," said Chief Petrovic. "Someone needs to do some legwork locating the lawyer and the will. Joel, I want you to pursue your idea and chase down that information."

The chief continued, "Cst. Jarvis, with the aid of that newspaper article you told us about, I want you to draft an advertisement that we could potentially run in the Toronto Evening Telegram. That should get the message out to most of Ontario. I also want the ad running in the three biggest papers in Illinois."

"When you have completed the draft of this notice, Jay, bring it to me," said Chief Petrovic.

Wednesday, March 29th

AT ABOUT 11 O'CLOCK Wednesday morning, I reported to Chief Petrovic that I had had some success in locating the last will and testament of the Featherstones.

I told the chief that I had contacted Henry Featherstone Monday afternoon. Henry was the only nephew of the Featherstones and he had become the owner of the Featherstone farm upon his father's death. Henry told me he did not have a copy of the will, but he knew that Old Mr. Prate had been the lawyer for the Featherstones.

"First thing Tuesday morning," I informed the chief, "I went to the office of Prate and Prate. Mr. Prate Senior is still alive, but he's in his late 80s and was no longer working in the office, so I spoke to his partner and son, Colin Prate, informing him that I was trying to locate copies of the wills of Harold and Marion Featherstone.

"Colin Prate got back to me first thing this morning. He located the will and told me that in the will there was a bequest to Henrietta Harriet Allenby of $1,000."

"That's great, Joel," said Chief Petrovic. "That's a significant financial incentive for anyone. I feel much more comfortable about placing the notice in the newspapers now. There'll be a quick meeting at 1:30 this afternoon for everyone to take a look at the notice to make certain there are no problems with it."

CHIEF PETROVIC STARTED the meeting by having me give everyone an update on the bequest that the Featherstones had left for Henny Allenby. Then he asked Jay to distribute copies of the notice he'd produced for the papers about the bequest. He passed them around and we all took a look:

Inheritance Bequest
Missing Heir

> A significant financial inheritance is available for Henrietta Harriet Allenby, who arrived in Canada in May 1901 as part of the British Home Child program. To qualify for the inheritance, Henrietta Harriet Allenby must present herself to the law firm of Wilson, Tome and Johnson at 186 Yonge Street, Toronto. Proof of identification is required.

After everyone had had a chance to read the notice, there was general agreement that Jay had done good work and that the notice was truthful.

"Cst. Herman, I think we're ready to send out the notice," said the chief. "I want you to contact the local paper. Tell them you want them to publish this notice and ask for their help in distributing it to the Toronto Evening Telegram and the three leading newspapers in Illinois. Don't discuss the notice any further with them. If they have any questions, they're to come and see me."

Tuesday, April 4th – Springfield, Illinois

HENNY MCCANN OPENED her front door, entered the foyer, took off her light jacket and hat, and put them in the front closet. Then she sat down on the deacon's bench and removed her boots and put on her slippers. It was a little after 4 o'clock in the afternoon and she had just returned from the bank. It was a very pleasant day for this early in April.

Henny planned to spend a quiet evening at home. After supper, she and her housekeeper, Millie, would discuss plans for the party Henny was hosting Saturday evening. For the moment, she just wanted a cup of tea and the Chicago Tribune. She could hear Millie fussing in the kitchen, busy preparing supper.

Henny sat down in her favourite chair in the living room and rang the little bell that was on the small end table placed beside her chair. Millie promptly appeared with a cup of tea and two freshly baked cookies. She placed the small tray on the table and quickly left the room to go back to the kitchen to finish preparing supper.

Henny opened the Chicago Tribune. She turned to the Society page first, as she usually did. She had an active social life and attended most of the society parties. She had cut way back on the drugs and alcohol of her earlier years, but she still enjoyed a good party. Henny was not extremely wealthy, but she was well off. She had married Dr. Frank McCann in 1914. He'd been ten years older than her. He hadn't seemed bothered that she didn't have any relatives. Dr. McCann had been a very prominent Chicago surgeon and had had many wealthy and influ-ential friends. He had died very suddenly about three and a half years after their marriage. Despite his early demise, Henny remained popular with the Chicago establishment. Frank's family had a history of heart trouble so there was no inquest into his death. Frank McCann had left Henny comfortably set for life.

Henny turned to the front page next. First Lady Eleanor Roosevelt, who had become the first American president's wife to hold her own press conferences, told reporters yesterday that beer would be served at the White House as soon as Prohibition ended. Mrs. Roosevelt empha-sized that she did not drink alcohol but that it would be available to guests of the President.

Spring training was just winding down for the Cubs and the White Sox, so the front page also had a short story predicting each team's chances of having a successful season. Last year the Cubs had won the National League pennant with a record of 90 wins and 64 losses, but they lost the World Series to the Yankees in four straight games. Great things were predicted for the Cubs. The White Sox were coming off a terrible season, where they'd only won 49 games. It was the worst sea-son in the history of the team. Dire predictions abounded for the 1933 season.

Henny still had a few minutes before suppertime, so she started to scan some of the other pages of the Tribune. The words 'missing heir' in a small article at the bottom of one of the pages caught her eye.

As Henny read through the short notice, she became more and more excited. She had heard a story from one of her acquaintances in Rockford about a young man who had suddenly been notified that an uncle had died and that he was the only heir. The young man had re-turned to England and soon became quite prosperous as the owner of a hat manufacturing company. It sounded a bit like a fairytale, but the acquaintance knew the man personally and had no reason to lie. These things happened. Henny McCann – formerly Henny Allenby but really Nancy Featherstone – believed that she led a charmed life and she was all in favour of getting more money.

There were a couple of minor inconveniences, of course. She would have to go to Canada, for starters, but she'd been there several times in the past ten years. She'd visited Toronto four times and Montréal several times as well. She would also have to prove that she was Henny Allenby. She could do that. When she had disposed of Henrietta Harriet Allenby, she had taken all of her personal belongings. That included all of her identification. In particular, it included the paperwork that had been filled out when Henny Allenby entered Canada.

But Henny had a Saturday night party to get ready for first. Aside from some of the hors d'oeuvres that Millie was preparing, Henny had also contacted one of Springfield's fancy restaurants for additional party food. The restaurant had also agreed to provide three waiters for Saturday evening.

Henny's home was large and she liked to show it off. Over sixty of Springfield's most important people had been invited. Even the mayor and his wife would be there. A three-piece band and a talented local singer would provide some live entertainment.

Once the party was out of the way, Henny planned to travel to Toronto to collect her inheritance. She would have Millie contact the train station first thing tomorrow morning to arrange first-class travel from Springfield to Chicago, then from Chicago to Detroit, and finally from Detroit to Toronto. If she left Springfield early Monday, she should be in Toronto sometime later in the day on Tuesday. Wednesday morning, she would visit the law offices of Wilson, Tome and Johnson on Young Street in Toronto to collect her inheritance.

Wednesday, April 12th

HENNY ALLENBY STEPPED out of the cab and glanced around. She thought, *I do like Toronto. Depending on how large an inheritance I've come to collect, I may purchase another home here.*

Toronto was a growing, modern city with a population of about 650,000; only 200,000 behind Montréal. The Toronto Islands, Henny thought, would be a great location for a home. The yacht club harbour was there and there were rumours about the construction of an airport on the island.

Henny was so caught up in her thoughts that she walked right by the door to the lawyer's office. She quickly realized her mistake, turned abruptly, and entered 186 Yonge Street. The receptionist was a prim, middle-age woman who looked extremely efficient and probably didn't have a sense of humour. The nameplate at the front of her desk said Maureen Thatcher.

"May I have your name, please," inquired the receptionist.

"Henrietta Harriet Allenby is my given name. Most people call me Henny."

"Which lawyer are you here to see?" asked Maureen.

"Oh, I don't have an appointment," replied Henny. Her manner seemed to suggest that she was too important to make appointments.

"Well, I'm not sure how we can help you," said the receptionist. "Please tell me the nature of your business, and then perhaps I can arrange to have one of the lawyers see you. If not today, then at their first available opportunity."

"I'm sorry. I'm not from Toronto and I'm not from Canada. I need to see someone today," answered Henny imperiously.

Frowning, the receptionist said, "I'll see what I can do, but you'll have to tell me the nature of your business first."

"I told you my name," said Henny, continuing in a too-important manner. "I'm surprised you didn't recognize it. You probably prepared the notice for the newspaper. You should pay more attention to your work."

The customer is always right, Maureen repeated to herself. *The customer is always right. I must be polite. I must be polite.* She took a deep breath and tried to smile. "You're right. I apologize. I didn't recognize you. We've been very busy. Do you have a copy of the newspaper notice?"

From her very expensive purse Henny produced her copy of the notice. "As you can see, and if you can hear," she added impolitely, "I am here about my inheritance."

"Yes, of course," said the receptionist. "Mr. Tome is looking after that matter. I'll get him for you now. You may have to wait for a few minutes. He's currently with another client."

"Thank you," said Henny somewhat mollified now by the apparent respectful manner of the receptionist.

About ten minutes later Mr. Tome appeared. He was a small, neat man in his mid-50s with a ready smile. He greeted Henny graciously and asked if she would accompany him to his office. He then called in the receptionist, Maureen, and asked that she prepare coffee for them. He also asked Maureen to walk over to the bakery down the street to purchase a couple of those excellent pastries they were famous for in Toronto.

Mr. Tome, who loved detective stories, had very efficiently used the ten minutes that Henny had spent waiting for him in the reception area. He had made two important telephone calls. The first call had been to Chief Petrovic in Chaseford.

When the chief had answered his phone, he'd heard a voice he didn't at first recognize say, somewhat mysteriously, "Hello, it's Tome. We have landed the fish."

Chief Petrovic had quickly caught on. "Make sure it's an allowable catch," he had said. "We don't want a problem with the game warden." After a brief pause Chief Petrovic had added, "Take some time to make sure that she has the proper credentials identifying her as Henrietta Harriet Allenby. Once you have verified her status, you may have to stall for time. I talked to the assistant chief in charge of detectives in Toronto last week. I'll call him now, as soon as I hang up. The assistant chief has promised to send someone promptly to your office."

Tome had waited three or four minutes and then phoned the Toronto police and asked for the assistant chief in charge of detectives. Tome had had to wait a couple of minutes before being put through to the assistant chief. As soon as he'd mentioned his name, the assistant chief had said, "I just finished talking to Chief Petrovic. I have one of my detectives and a police officer on the way to your office."

"I do love those pastries," said Mr. Tome after Maureen had left. "I'm sure you'll enjoy them."

This fellow seems a very pleasant gentleman, thought Henny. *I wonder if he's married.* She said, "You're very thoughtful, Mr. Tome. I'm certain the pastries will be delightful."

"Well, I guess we'd better get down to business," Tome said. "I'll need to see some sort of identification. We wouldn't want to give the money to the wrong person." He chuckled.

Henny smiled back at him, chuckling as well. "Oh, I'm the right person," she said. "Here's a copy of the letter sent to Harold and Marion Featherstone from the Central Registry files of the Immigration branch of the Canadian government verifying my arrival in Toronto. They picked me up in Toronto in May of 1901. I was only 11 years old at the time. The world was a very confusing place to me, but the Featherstones were very good to me. When I heard that they had disappeared I was devastated."

Mr. Tome looked at her sympathetically, disguising his feelings as best he could. He was very good at it. He had been acting in courtrooms in Toronto for many years. "Do you have any current identification?" he inquired.

Henny produced her Illinois driver's license and her American passport. Mr. Tome took his time examining them.

"Well, everything seems to be in order here," he said finally. "I need to step out of the office for a moment. If the receptionist returns with the pastries before I get back, please help yourself." He smiled and left.

A moment later there was a knock on the door and two men entered the room. One was obviously a policeman in uniform, the other one just behaved like a policeman. Henny was startled. She had been expecting either Mr. Tome or the receptionist. She didn't know what to think. She wasn't left wondering for long.

The plainclothes man said, "I'm Detective Pilsner. You are under arrest for the murder of Henrietta Harriet Allenby." He then started to read Henny her rights. He only got about four words out before she started screaming loudly.

"You're out of your mind! I just proved to the lawyer a few minutes ago, in this very office, that I am Henrietta Harriet Allenby. I am quite clearly alive. I certainly didn't kill myself."

While she was screaming, the uniform policeman cuffed her. The immediate effect of which was louder ranting. Det. Pilsner waited her out. When she paused for breath he read her rights to her.

"Do you want to leave the building quietly or do you want the two of us to carry you out to the cruiser?" said Det. Pilsner.

"I'll go with you," she said, "but you're making a big mistake. This is total nonsense. I'm not talking to anybody until I get a lawyer."

Henny quieted down. The two policemen took her out into the reception room. She started screaming again when she saw Tome and the receptionist drinking coffee and eating those 'special pastries' that Tome had promised her. The policemen forced her out through the front door of 186 Yonge Street and into the cruiser. It was not a pleasant ride to the police station.

AS SOON AS THE PHONE call with Tome ended, Chief Petrovic brought Cst. Herman into the office. "I know you love to drive, Peter," the chief said, smiling.

"That smile tells me that something good has happened," said Cst. Herman.

"Our plan is working," said the chief. "Henny Allenby, a.k.a. Nancy Featherstone, or, according to her latest identification, Henny McCann, saw the newspaper notice and crossed the border to Toronto from the US to collect her inheritance." Then he added, almost muttering, showing his frustration, "It's a wonder she can keep track of herself. One or two more aliases and we would probably never have caught her."

"When do we leave?" asked Cst. Herman.

"I think we should leave now," said Chief Petrovic. "It will take us at least two and a half hours to get to Toronto. Let's allow three hours by the time we get to the Toronto police station and locate Henny. It's about 10:30 in the morning right now. If we do leave now, and stop for an hour for lunch in Hamilton, we should get to the Toronto police Station about 2:30 this afternoon."

"Are we going to interview her in Toronto, Chief?" asked Cst. Herman.

"No, I want to bring her back to Chaseford. That's closer to the scene of her crimes. Maybe that will upset her. I know she won't feel bad. I don't think she's capable of remorse," said Chief Petrovic. "But maybe it will shake her up."

"So, we get the pleasure of her company all the way back?" asked Cst. Herman.

"Yes. Aren't you happy that I had that heavy screening installed between the front seat and the back seat?" replied the chief. "Let's go get in the car."

CHIEF PETROVIC AND Cst. Herman pulled into the parking lot of the Toronto police station a little after 2:15 in the afternoon. They'd had a decent lunch at a place in Hamilton that Chief O'Donnell had recommended to them. The last part of their trip to the Toronto police station had taken less than an hour, so they were not road-weary.

The Chief and Cst. Herman thought they were prepared for their brief meeting at the Toronto police station. They would take custody of the prisoner, now formally identified as Henny McCann, and transport her to Chaseford. As they waited at the desk, however, they could hear quite a tumult behind the closed doors of a hallway to their left.

Suddenly, the doors burst open and a woman in restraints was carried towards them by two burly policemen. The woman, at a very high volume, was shouting something that sounded like, "Toronto Secret Police", and "Nazi pigs", laced profusely with profanities that seemed to increase in volume and vulgarity the closer she approached the desk.

"Package for the Chaseford police," shouted one of the policemen. He could scarcely be heard above the screaming vitriol spewing from the bundled prisoner. "We'd like to complete this exchange as soon as possible," the policeman shouted. "The assistant chief told us that, if you so wished, we could place her in your vehicle for you once the transfer paperwork is complete."

"We would appreciate that," shouted Chief Petrovic. He took the policeman aside so they could speak at a normal volume. "Has she been screaming like this long?" he asked.

"Only since she was apprehended, Chief," answered the policeman with a smile.

With the paperwork completed and the packaged prisoner installed in the back of the police car – behind the protective screen – Chief Petrovic and Cst. Herman reluctantly climbed into the front of the cruiser. They didn't know what to expect during the trip back to Chaseford.

THE FIRST FORTY-FIVE minutes of the trip was torture. Chief Petrovic and Cst. Herman had agreed beforehand not to respond to her shouting in any obvious manner. At times, the desire to gag her or slap her was almost overwhelming. Instead, they stopped the car and got out about every ten minutes to take a break. Eventually, the shouting began to die down. It was replaced by a continuous litany of demands. This noise level was easier to ignore.

By the time they reached Chaseford there was only an occasional demand or comment from the rear seat of the car. Henny seemed to have calmed down considerably. The chief and Cst. Herman had weathered the storm, although they did have serious headaches.

It was about 6 o'clock when they reached the police station in Chaseford. "I want both constables Jarvis and Franklin here before we remove her from the car," said Chief Petrovic. "You stay with the car Peter, while I go and make a couple of phone calls. You can get out of the car if you wish."

Cst. Jay Jarvis and Cst. Joel Franklin were at the police station within fifteen minutes. When they arrived, the chief looked at them and said, "I'm sorry to interrupt your evening, but we may need your help. So far Henny's been a very difficult prisoner. Incidentally, she was married a few years ago. Her name is now legally Henny McCann."

Constables Jarvis and Franklin said nothing but thought that, at the moment, Henny appeared calm and rested whereas Chief Petrovic and Cst. Herman appeared haggard. They knew better than to ask about the trip.

Chief Petrovic pointed at Jay and Joel and said, "You two are taking her the next time she needs to be escorted somewhere." The chief appeared to be grumpy.

Cst. Jarvis and Cst. Franklin were able to escort Henny McCann to her cell, where they removed her restraints without any problem. When they told her that she would receive her supper within half an hour, she responded, "Thank you very much. I'm quite hungry. I didn't get any lunch. You two are the nicest policemen I've ever met."

She said this within earshot of Chief Petrovic and Cst. Herman. They looked at each other in astonishment.

"Is that the same person we met at the Toronto police station and escorted to Chaseford?" Chief Petrovic asked Cst. Herman.

"The change in behaviour is amazing," answered the constable. "She seems like a different person."

Thursday, April 13th

"IT'S BEEN MORE THAN four months since that first body part came to our attention back in December," said Chief Petrovic. "At the beginning, it seemed like an almost impossible case to solve. But we kept working, doing lots of legwork, and following up on lots of leads. Now we have a suspect locked up in one of our cells. But this certainly isn't a *simple* case. We still don't have the bodies of the murder victims. The body parts we discovered are beyond the capabilities of forensic science to identify. I wonder how many more murders our suspect has committed? What really happened to her husband, Dr. McCann, for instance?"

"Aside from the confession she made to Johnnie Polizzi and Ernie Stanzio when she was high on drugs, what real evidence do we have?" asked Cst. Smith.

"None, really. But Henny McCann is a complex person," said the chief. "I wanted to get her back to Chaseford because I think when she's confronted in an interview, even with the limited evidence we have, because we have the recorded testimony from Polizzi and Stanzio, we'll get a confession."

We looked at Chief Petrovic skeptically.

"Remember, we've seen two very different sides of her personality. On Wednesday, when she was arrested in Toronto, she became a raving, wild, ungovernable person. The police in Toronto had to put her in restraints to carry her to our car. It was all Cst. Herman and I could do to put up with her screaming rant all the way back to Chaseford. I think

135

the person that Cst. Herman and I saw on the trip behaved like Nancy Featherstone. I think that's the person that murdered her parents and Henrietta Allenby.

"But since she arrived at our jail last night she's been a model prisoner. She's been pleasant and agreeable. I think that's the way Henny McCann behaves.

"Constables Smith, Jarvis, and Franklin, you haven't seen her when she's in a state of rage. Regardless of her current behavior, be extremely cautious when you're around her. I believe she's capable of anything.

"As you are aware, we have not interviewed her yet. She will only speak to us about the charges in the presence of her lawyer. She is a wealthy woman and consequently she has hired the best criminal defense lawyer in Ontario, Fred Donaldson. He has an office in Toronto. He will be present for our first interview with her at 1:30 this afternoon. Cst. Herman and I will conduct the interview. Peter and I will take the rest of the morning to get prepared. This morning's meeting is over."

FOUR PEOPLE SAT AT the table in Chief Petrovic's office. Cst. Herman and Chief Petrovic sat on one side of the table; across from them sat the lawyer, Fred Donaldson, and the accused, Henny McCann. The chief and the lawyer had agreed that the chief's office was the best place to conduct the interviews. Donaldson further stipulated that no one else could be present in the interview room except for the recording secretary, Sherry Simpson, the police chief's secretary, who was going to act as the recording secretary for the interviews. Sherry understood she was legally bound by the rules of confidentiality to reveal nothing about the interviews. Sherry was seated at a small table at one end of the room where she was visible to all four participants.

Chief Petrovic started the interview by asking the accused to identify herself.

"I'm Henny McCann, an American citizen from Springfield, Illinois," said Henny.

"Was your maiden name Henrietta Harriet Allenby?" asked the chief.

"That was my maiden name," Henny confirmed. "I identified myself using that name at the law office of Wilson, Tome and Johnson on Yonge Street in Toronto. I had papers that proved my identity. I am eligible for the inheritance."

Chief Petrovic ignored the last couple comments. He did not want to upset her. He suspected that, if that happened, she would become irrational.

Before he could ask his next question, Chief Petrovic was interrupted by the lawyer. Donaldson opened his briefcase and pulled out a newspaper clipping. It was a copy of the notice that had been placed in the newspapers under the title 'Missing Heir.'

"Is this inheritance legitimate or was this notice just a ploy to entrap my client?" Donaldson asked.

The chief looked Donaldson in the eye and responded, "It's a legitimate inheritance from the estate of Harold and Marion Featherstone. They were a prominent local family. We also wanted to speak to her about a murder investigation we're conducting."

"Well then, I think arrangements should be made so that she can obtain her rightful inheritance. Then she can leave your jail, leave Canada, and return to her home in Springfield, Illinois," Donaldson said authoritatively.

"Oh, I don't think it's that straightforward," said Chief Petrovic. "There seems to be some doubt as to whether she really is Henny McCann."

"That's preposterous," exclaimed Donaldson. "I've looked at her identification. All of it identifies her as Henny McCann, wife of former prominent surgeon, Dr. Frank McCann, of Springfield, Illinois."

"Well, I have two sworn affidavits from American citizens that she is Nancy Featherstone, born just outside of Chaseford, Ontario," answered Chief Petrovic.

That's when the screaming started. Henny leaped up, sprawling across the table, and put both of her hands around Chief Petrovic's throat, clamping her teeth around one of his ears. Sherry Simpson started screaming. Donaldson and Cst. Herman jumped to their feet and each took hold of one of Henny's hands, trying to pull them from around the chief's neck. It was chaos.

The men shouted at Henny, trying to get her to release the chief's ear, but she simply snarled. All of a sudden, there was a tremendously loud bang. Henny screamed, releasing the chief, and he backed away, his ear damaged but whole. There was a fair bit of blood.

There was a temporary lull and then Henny resumed her shrieking, repeating ferociously, *"You're all evil! I will make you pay! I'll get you all! You'll pay with your lives!"* Interspersed among these phrases were profanities and other garbled sentences that no one could decipher.

By this time, the other three constables had arrived in the office. Cst. Franklin and Cst. Jarvis managed to get Henny's hands behind her back and handcuffed her.

"Sorry for discharging my firearm in your office, Chief," yelled Cst. Smith above the uproar from Henny. "There's some minor damage above your window from the bullet. I thought the noise might startle her and give the rest of us a chance to intervene."

Henny's full-volume rant continued as she was taken down the hallway to her cell. Five minutes ago, they'd been conducting a formal interview in a routine fashion; now everyone was in a state of shock. Chief Petrovic sat at the table, carefully inspecting his ear, while Sherry Simpson leaned against one of the filing cabinets, eyes and mouth wide open. The lawyer, Donaldson, now quite pale and momentarily speechless, was once more sitting down at the table across from Chief Petrovic.

Chief Petrovic said, "I think you should take the rest the day off, Sherry. See how you feel after the weekend. If you can't return Monday, let me know. But remember, this is all confidential."

Cst. Herman roused himself and escorted Sherry Simpson from the room.

Chief Petrovic and Fred Donaldson were now alone in the office. "I was hoping this wouldn't happen," said Chief Petrovic, "although I knew there was a chance it could. Cst. Herman and I have seen Henny like this before. It can last for hours. When she's in this state, you can't really communicate with her. But when she returns to normal, you can talk to her in a civilized manner. It's almost like she's two different people."

"Henny paid me a very large retainer," said Fred Donaldson, "so I will continue to represent her, but this outburst of abnormal behaviour requires some research and some additional consideration of the facts surrounding the case. She definitely needs medical attention. I'll contact a psychiatrist I know and then either he or someone he recommends can visit her. I'm finished here today, Chief Petrovic. I'll get in touch with you later."

Wednesday, April 19th

WEDNESDAY MORNING, at 10 o'clock, Chief Petrovic had a brief meeting with his constables. The chief started the meeting by saying, "I want all of you available in the police station at 2 o'clock this afternoon."

The constables looked at one another, uncertain about why they all needed to be present. The chief had never made a request like this before.

Chief Petrovic continued, "I received a phone call late yesterday afternoon from Dr. Alfred Khryscoff, the doctor the lawyer Donaldson indicated he would get in touch with to meet with Henny McCann. Dr. Khryscoff is a prominent psychiatrist with an office in Toronto. He said visiting Henny at 2 o'clock this afternoon would work out very well for him, since he has relatives in London he's been meaning to visit. He plans on travelling to London after he's finished his interview with Henny."

The constables immediately understood why Chief Petrovic wanted all of them in the building that afternoon.

"Oh, by the way," the chief said, "I've given Sherry Simpson the afternoon off."

DR. ALFRED KHRYSCOFF arrived at the chief's office at about half past one and introduced himself to Chief Petrovic. Khryscoff was a bear of a man. He was at least six foot two and had a beard that still showed traces of red, despite a full head of graying hair. The chief placed his age at around 50.

"I am so pleased to meet you," Dr. Khryscoff said. "From my acquaintance, Mr. Donaldson, I understand that you have a difficult prisoner. How has her behaviour been since the event that so engraved itself on my friend's mind?"

"Henny carried on in that lovely, strident voice of hers at full volume for about two hours after Mr. Donaldson left the building," said the chief. "She has remarkable stamina. The incident was last Friday afternoon and since then she has been a model prisoner. I told Henny at suppertime yesterday that you would be coming to see her this afternoon. I told her you were an acquaintance of her lawyer. I wasn't sure what else to say, so I left it at that."

"You handled that well, Chief Petrovic," said Dr. Khryscoff. "Henny and I will have a conversation, and as we are talking I'll introduce myself in a nonthreatening way. I'm glad I wasn't here on Friday, but I have been involved in similar incidents. I understand she attacked your ears with more than just loud noises. I would guess it took about five stitches to close that wound."

"It's healing very well. It took seven stitches. Unfortunately, it didn't affect my hearing," responded Chief Petrovic with a wry smile.

"I'm ready to speak to her," said Dr. Khryscoff. "It would be best if I spoke to her by myself. You can post a man outside the door. Do you have a room that I can use that provides a more pleasant environment than her cell?"

"There aren't a lot of pleasant rooms in this building, Dr. Khryscoff," replied the chief. "However, we do have a supply room that is currently almost empty. There's a large window in it that looks out on the park across the street. There's a table in there, and I can easily arrange to have a couple of chairs placed in the room. Let's take a look."

The two of them got up and went to the adjacent room. Dr. Khryscoff looked around the supply room. He turned, and said, "Would it be okay to move the table closer to the window?"

"That's not a problem. I'll help you," said Chief Petrovic.

Within five minutes, two chairs had been moved into the room and it was ready for Dr. Khryscoff and Henny McCann to have their conversation.

"Cst. Joel Franklin is the policeman that will be posted outside your door for the interview," said Chief Petrovic as he left.

I WAS THE LUCKY CONSTABLE who drew first watch duty outside the door to the supply room. From my location, Dr. Khryscoff and Henny McCann's voices were clearly audible. They had been in conversation for several minutes. Khryscoff had introduced himself, and, in a low-key manner, had explained that he was a doctor of psychiatry and that he was working for her lawyer on her behalf. He said it was necessary for her lawyer to understand how Henny thought if he was going to successfully represent her. I noticed that he chose his words very carefully. He did not say 'defend' her. He said 'represent' her. I assumed that Dr. Khryscoff was concerned and chose words that would not trigger an outburst.

After the introductory conversation, I was surprised at Dr. Khryscoff's first question.

"What is your name?" he asked Henny.

There was a pause. She said, apparently not offended, "You're being silly, Doctor. You know my name."

"I'm sorry," he said. "I mean would you spell your name for me please."

She spelled out Henrietta Harriet McCann for the doctor.

His next question was just as confusing to me. Dr. Khryscoff asked, "Do you ever feel like you're someone else?"

WHERE'S THE REST OF THE BODY?   143

"What do you mean doctor?" she asked.

"Are you aware that you have episodes when you scream and rage for hours?" he asked.

"Don't be silly," she said. "Who's been telling you stories?"

"Why are you here in this jail?" he said as his next question.

"I'm not sure," Henny said. "I think it's got something to do with my papers. I remember going to the lawyer's office in Toronto to collect my rightful inheritance. I remember presenting my papers. They were legitimate. The lawyer left the room. The police came in and I don't remember anything after that."

"Do you remember your car ride here?"

"I do not. I slept all the way," Henny responded.

I thought I could now detect some agitation in Henny's responses.

"How do you feel now?" asked Dr. Khryscoff.

"I'm becoming upset," said Henny.

Dr. Khryscoff then asked, "Do you know someone by the name of Millie?"

"Yes, Millie is my live-in housekeeper in Springfield, Illinois. She's a good person. She's been very helpful to me," answered Henny.

He must have sensed her agitation. Maybe this question was to calm her down. It may have. But before I could think about it much he asked the next question.

"Who is Nancy Featherstone?" Dr. Khryscoff asked.

I heard something almost like a growl, the banging of furniture being toppled, and then intense screaming. I raced into the room and found Dr. Khryscoff doing his best to hold onto Henny McCann's arms. He was a large strong man but in her insane mood she was a match for him. I grabbed her right arm and pulled it behind her back. Dr. Khryscoff managed to move her left arm behind her back as well so that she could be handcuffed.

Once again, the police station – and probably the surrounding buildings – were subjected to extremely loud yelling and cursing and words that made no sense.

By the time Dr. Khryscoff and I had Henny on her feet and to the door of the supply room, Chief Petrovic had arrived, followed closely by the other constables. Cst. Smith and Cst. Jarvis took custody of Henny and dragged her back to her cell. Chief Petrovic excused Cst. Herman and me and then the chief and Dr. Khryscoff retired to his office for a private conversation.

"WELL DOCTOR, WHAT DO you think?" asked the chief.

"There's not much doubt in my mind, Chief Petrovic," Dr. Khryscoff responded. "This woman has a lot of the classic symptoms of multiple personality disorder. It's a form of dissociation. It may be too early to tell, but I'm sure she has at least two personalities. From what little I know," Dr. Khryscoff continued, "Henny McCann seems like a fairly normal, middle-aged, well-to-do woman who usually gets what she wants. The other personality is likely Nancy Featherstone. You did tell me a little bit about her when we first met. Nancy sounds like an uncontrolled, murderous psychopath who stops at nothing to get her way. I prefer Henny," he said and chuckled.

"Despite this woman's mental problems," said Chief Petrovic, "I need to pursue this case to its conclusion in order to provide a sense of relief and security to the relatives of the deceased and to this community. This is not just a pretty speech; this 'body parts' murder case has dominated the local news and gossip since last December."

"I understand your concerns," said Dr. Khryscoff. "But you have to appreciate that Henny McCann is not a murderer."

At this point the chief interrupted him. "You can argue that. There may even be some validity to the idea. But people were murdered and someone has to be held accountable."

"I'll leave you and Fred Donaldson to chew on that for a while," said Dr. Khryscoff. "I don't want you to have to continually deal with the other uncontrollable part of Henny's personality. I'll write a prescription for a tranquilizer. That should damp down her uncontrollable rage. Henny may not like the effects of the medication, but it is for her own good."

WHEN I GOT BACK TO my lodgings at the back of Franklin's Groceries, Georgie was there waiting. I'm not sure whether I said "Oops" or "Hi" first. I was supposed to have met Georgie at 5 o'clock. We were going out to supper at Mabel's Diner. It was now a little after 5:30, so an apology was in order.

After I apologized, Georgie said, "That's very nice of you, but it's not necessary. I gather there was another noisy disturbance at the police station this afternoon. Downtown, people said they could hear shouting and yelling half a block away. The rumour is you have a lunatic locked up."

"Remember Georgie, anything I say to you is totally confidential," I answered. "The person isn't a lunatic but depending on their mood they can be dangerous. We had a psychiatrist at the police station today to visit her. His name is Dr. Khryscoff. I stood guard outside the door while he met with the prisoner alone in an interview room. It's the first time I've ever met a psychiatrist. I was very impressed with the way he handled the interview. He obviously has a lot of experience working with people with mental abnormalities and it got me to thinking. Dr. Khryscoff might be someone I should talk to about my abilities."

"Do you think that's a good idea, Joel?" asked Georgie. "Do you think you can trust him?"

"I believe I can," I responded. "He's bound by the doctor-patient confidentiality part of his oath."

"If you make an appointment, could I go with you?" asked Georgie.

"I wouldn't have it any other way," I said. "I asked Dr. Khryscoff for his phone number just before he left the police station."

Thursday, April 20th

CHIEF PETROVIC THOUGHT he was ready for his meeting with the lawyer, Fred Donaldson. They had agreed to meet at the chief's office at 2 o'clock, on Thursday afternoon. Donaldson had stayed in town overnight at the Chaseford Arms Hotel and was travelling back to Toronto the following day.

The meeting was just a few minutes away and the chief was of two minds. Chief Petrovic did not like defence lawyers. To him, they always seemed to be twisting the truth, so he felt certain that Donaldson would try to twist his words to create an advantage for the accused. At the same time, he was anxious to push the case forward. Chief Petrovic thought he had the guilty party locked up and enough circumstantial evidence to convict Henny McCann of murder. Although it was extremely unsettling that Henny McCann sometimes seemed to be someone else.

Sherry Simpson peeked around the corner the door and said, "Fred Donaldson is here to see you."

The chief was pleased to see that Sherry had regained some of her spunk after the upset she had experienced witnessing Henny's violent outburst.

"Tell him I'll just be a moment," answered Chief Petrovic. He took a couple of reports off the meeting table and put them in his desk drawer. Then he went to the door and welcomed Donaldson into his office.

"You're looking good," said Donaldson. "Even that ear seems to be in a good state of repair."

"It hasn't improved my hearing, but thank you for noticing. And for agreeing to meet with me so soon," said the chief. "You're probably as anxious as I am to resolve this situation. I gather you've had a conversation with Dr. Khryscoff too."

"I have," answered Donaldson. "I think we have three different agendas for the same person. You want to get a murder conviction; I want to defend her because I think Henny McCann is innocent of the charge; Dr. Khryscoff sees a patient he needs to treat. There must be some common ground somewhere."

Chief Petrovic was surprised by Donaldson's opening statement. He had anticipated a flat rejection of any attempt to move away from a plain 'not guilty' result. He supposed that Donaldson had had a bit of a wake-up when he'd been front row and centre for Henny McCann's violent rampage. "Do you have any suggestions, Mr. Donaldson?" asked the chief.

"I was afraid if the matter was left to the two of us, we would never resolve it," Donaldson answered. "So I asked Dr. Khryscoff for his opinion. He refused to attend our meeting, but he did give me his thoughts in writing. The doctor was staying at the Chaseford Arms as well, so he gave me this letter before he checked out this morning." Donaldson put the letter down on the table so that the chief could read it.

Gentlemen,

I know we all have different agendas, but all of us are bound to serve the community and private individuals to the best of our ability. Henny McCann, in her present state of health, is a danger to the community. She needs to be confined to a mental institution where she can be treated for her illness. It's possible Henny may never again be healthy enough to return to society. That's unfortunate for Henny, because I believe the guilty party in this case is Nancy Featherstone. If we can deal with the Nancy Featherstone part of Henny McCann in an institution-

al setting, perhaps Henny may be cured and can become a person capable of living in society again.

The community also deserves consideration. We must make every reasonable attempt to determine what really happened. The public is entitled to know the truth. Relatives and friends and those immediately involved in the case need to have some closure.

I am not opposed to a guilty verdict provided there is no death penalty and that Henny McCann will be eligible for consideration for probation if she is cured of her mental affliction and is deemed capable of functioning as a normal person in society.

Sincerely,

Dr. Alfred Khryscoff

The two men looked at each other without saying a word.

"After witnessing Henny's behavior, both as herself and at other times – perhaps – as Nancy Featherstone, I'm willing to accept that Dr. Khryscoff's suggestion may be the most manageable way to handle this case," said Chief Petrovic.

"I agree with you," said Donaldson. "I think it is necessary, though, that the case be taken before a judge and not a jury."

"I'll talk to the judge," said the chief. "Geoffrey Bernard. He's been on the job here for a little over two years. He was appointed when Judge Marshall retired. If you're in agreement, I'll take the letter from Dr. Khryscoff. I think it will help."

"Please keep me informed about the results of your meeting with the judge. I'll also need to know the trial date as soon as possible," said Donaldson.

Monday, April 24th

CHIEF PETROVIC HAD an appointment for 10 o'clock Monday morning with Judge Bernard. Geoffrey Bernard was about ten years younger than the chief, in his mid-40s. He was a little on the pudgy side, but his eyes betrayed a keen intelligence. Bernard had only been in the area for a little over two years, but he already had a reputation as being fair in his dealings. He was a good listener but once he started to speak you were to be quiet.

Chief Petrovic was invited to sit in front of the judge's desk. After their exchange of greetings, the judge said, "What matter do you bring forward to me today, Chief Petrovic?"

"Your Honor, I haven't discussed this case with you before," said the chief. "It's been complicated, but it's reached the point where I have a suspect and as much evidence as I think I'll be able to accumulate."

"OK, Chief Petrovic. Start at the beginning and give me as many of the details as you can," said Judge Bernard.

Chief Petrovic started his presentation by describing the sudden appearance of the body parts in December. He went on to relate the discovery of the icehouse on the Featherstone farm, and then continued by describing how he had obtained two witnesses from the United States. He then told the judge about the notice in the newspapers and finished by describing Henny's arrest and behaviour. The recitation took the better part of an hour.

When Chief Petrovic stopped, Judge Bernard looked at him with those penetrating eyes and said, "This is certainly a most unusual case. I am concerned about the mental well-being of the suspect, Henny Mc-Cann, and I'm very pleased that you involved someone as prominent as Dr. Khryscoff to assess her. Do you have any recommendations for me Chief Petrovic?"

"This was not an easy situation to deal with," answered Chief Petrovic. "Henny McCann is quite a wealthy woman and she hired Fred Donaldson to serve as her lawyer."

The judge interjected, "I have not had Mr. Donaldson in my courtroom before, but from everything I have heard he's an excellent defense attorney and usually gets his way. This may not be easy."

"Mr. Donaldson and I have had a couple of discussions," said Chief Petrovic. "Our last meeting went better than I anticipated. He knows Dr. Khryscoff very well and respects him. We both agreed to invite Dr. Khryscoff to our last meeting, but the doctor declined to attend. Instead, he wrote a letter stating his opinion, which he gave Donaldson to present to me at our meeting. I would appreciate it if you would read Dr. Khryscoff's letter."

Chief Petrovic handed the letter to the judge.

Judge Bernard took the letter and read it carefully. "What did you and Donaldson think of the letter?" he said when he had finished.

"Much to our mutual surprise, we both agreed that it presented a reasonable solution to a difficult problem," responded the chief.

"I feel much better now than I did ten minutes ago, when you first mentioned Donaldson's name," said Judge Bernard. "Just sit and relax for a few moments. I'm going to fetch our local prosecuting attorney, Howard Wainwright. He needs to be here for the last part of this meeting."

Wainwright appeared five minutes later and sat down beside Chief Petrovic, in front of the judge's desk. The judge asked the chief to repeat his story, but to use a condensed version, adding that he would present any other necessary details to Wainwright later. When Chief Petrovic had finished, the judge asked Wainwright to read the letter from Dr. Khryscoff, which the prosecuting attorney did very carefully.

When he'd finished, the judge asked Wainwright if he had any questions. He did. The judge and Chief Petrovic answered the questions as well as they could.

Judge Bernard then said, "Here's how I see this case unfolding: We will use Dr. Khryscoff's recommendations as the basis for the resolution of the murder case. I want a plea bargain whereby Henny McCann pleads guilty to murder but the court agrees that there are extenuating circumstances due to diminished mental capacity. There will be no sentence of execution for murder; rather, Henny McCann's sentence will result in incarceration in a secure psychiatric hospital for the remainder of her life, or until she is determined to be cured by the hospital staff. If she is pronounced cured, she will be eligible to apply for probation. Further, there will be a full inquest into the deaths of the Featherstones.

"This plea bargain is contingent upon the accused Henny McCann providing as much cooperation as she possibly can in answering questions surrounding the deaths of the Featherstones and the disappearance of Nancy Featherstone.

"Mr. Wainwright, I will have the plea bargain written out for you," said Judge Bernard. "Once you have it in your hands, I want you to have a meeting with Mr. Donaldson. If there are any concerns or questions from Mr. Donaldson, please let me know. Minor changes you can make as you see fit."

Wednesday, April 26th

WEDNESDAY AT LUNCH time I dropped over to the Chaseford General Hospital to have a brief visit with Georgie. She had a one-hour lunch break starting at 12:30, and as our wedding was little more than a month away, we had some details to discuss. I also wanted to tell her about my phone call to Dr. Khryscoff the previous night.

It was a beautiful April day. Winter was almost forgotten. Greenery was starting to appear everywhere. Georgie and I sat on the rear steps of the hospital.

"What's new?" I said.

"My mother and I are almost frantic over these wedding preparations," and Georgie.

We chatted about wedding preparations, what guests would be coming, and our friends and relatives for a few minutes. As that part of our conversation wound down, I said, "Remember I called Dr. Khryscoff last Thursday night about setting up an appointment to see him? He called me back this morning. It turns out he'll be in town late this afternoon. He's doing another assessment of Henny McCann tomorrow, so he decided to come to town today and stay overnight at the Chaseford Arms. He volunteered to see me this evening if it's convenient for me. I asked if he'd like to come to my place. I told him it wasn't fancy. I also mentioned that you'd like to be there. Can you come over tonight?"

"Joel, that sounds great," said Georgie. "I'm a little nervous about you confiding in someone else, but you seem to be confident he's a good man. Someone we can trust. I think we should play the 'guess that card' game sometime during the evening."

"I'm not so sure about that," I replied. "I don't know Dr. Khryscoff well enough to even guess how he might feel about that type of demonstration. It almost seems like showing off."

"I think it's more like proof of your ability," said Georgie. "He might be quite intrigued by the demonstration." We were by ourselves, so Georgie gave me a kiss and said, "I have to get back to the nursing station. I'll be at your place by 6:45 tonight."

PROMPTLY AT SEVEN THERE was a knock on the door.

I opened it. "Welcome to my fancy abode," I said. "This is my fiancée, Georgie Harkness."

"I'm very pleased to meet you, Georgie," said Dr. Khryscoff. "You are a beautiful young woman and Joel is a lucky young man."

Georgie blushed but recovered quickly. "I keep telling him that," she said. We all laughed and with the laughter immediately felt comfortable with one another.

"I offer you my only comfortable chair, Doctor. Would you like a small glass of red wine?" I handed the bottle to Dr. Khryscoff so he could examine the label.

"Oh, this is a very good wine," said the doctor. "I would be delighted to have some."

I poured the wine and we seated ourselves around my small table. There was just enough room for our wine glasses and Dr. Khryscoff's notebook.

"From your brief comments the other day, Joel, I think you have a story to tell me," said the doctor.

"You could say that."

I told the doctor about the lightning strike and about my encounter with Walter. Then I told him about Louise Carter and about

Walter's role in helping me save Cst. Herman's life. I did not tell him Gwen Cumming's name. During the entire time that I spoke, Dr. Khryscoff did not interrupt me once.

When I'd finished, he looked at me and said, "You don't look crazy."

He saw the expression on my face and roared with laughter.

"I'm teasing you, Joel," he said. "Implausible as this story may sound to many people, I believe you. The human mind is a strange entity. We still don't know how it works or what it's capable of. I have dealt with a lot of people who have had strange experiences. Most of those experiences are due to hallucination, but I think some extremely sensitive people do have experiences that most people have no understanding of. And of course, you know the unknown is a frightening thing, so these events are sometimes dismissed as the creations of an unhealthy mind."

I relaxed and smiled back at the doctor. "Thank you," I said.

"I'd like Joel to do a demonstration for you, Doctor. If he's agreeable and if you are interested."

Dr. Khryscoff gave Georgie an inquisitive look. "Tell me what the demonstration involves."

Georgie explained the game. I got up and went around to the other side of the wall of goods, out of sight of both Georgie and Dr. Khryscoff. I had a pad of paper and a pencil with me so that I could record the identities of the cards that Dr. Khryscoff would draw from the deck. The doctor remained on the other side of the wall at the table with his notebook and pen and a deck of cards. We had agreed to a trial of ten cards.

Dr. Khryscoff began to draw cards. After I had recorded my guess for the tenth card, I walked back around the wall to the room where Georgie and Dr. Khryscoff were sitting and joined them at the table. The doctor had his list tucked in his shirt pocket. I handed him my list. He looked at it, but his expression didn't give anything away.

He handed me his list. When I looked at it, I was somewhat disappointed as I had only scored seven out of ten.

"Scoring seven out of ten is certainly far above random guessing," I said. "But I'm disappointed. I thought I would do better."

"I'm not disappointed," said the doctor. "I'm amazed. Joel, you were correct on all seven of the cards I concentrated on. The one card I didn't look at you got wrong. The remaining two cards I looked at but didn't concentrate on. It's still surprising. One of the cards was the three of clubs. You wrote down two of clubs. The other card was the jack of diamonds. You wrote down jack of hearts. Your ability is certainly amazing. I have never seen anything like it. But I have never talked to anyone like you before. I've talked to charlatans, to magicians, and to other sleight-of-hand artists. None of the ones I have met have this kind of ability."

I sat there dumbfounded. I knew I had a talent but now I knew it was special. It felt good to have a renowned psychiatrist tell me he believed in me. For the first time, I felt confident in my ability.

"I think he's speechless," said Georgie. "Doctor, can you show me how you made him speechless? I may want to be able to do this at some point after we're married."

We all laughed.

"Thank you very much, Doctor," I said. "It's wonderful to know that other people have some faith in your ability."

"I think it's important that I also tell you this, Dr. Khryscoff," said Georgie. "Joel's ability extends beyond identifying cards. He and I have also discovered that, depending on the situation, Joel can almost read someone's mind if they are highly wrought. He can also quite accurately predict what they may physically do next."

"I'm not totally surprised by that," said the doctor. "From what you said earlier, Joel, you and Walter believe that when a person is concentrating or under duress their brain sends or broadcasts a weak electromagnetic signal. I'm not ready to believe that. I'm not even certain we have the scientific know-how to measure that signal. But we do know that there are obvious physical signals or body language that a person in distress exhibits. That's another possible explanation for mind-reading, though certainly not for guessing cards correctly."

"I know Joel won't ask," said Georgie, "but I will. Can Joel attend your interview with Henny McCann? I think he could be helpful."

There was a long pause. I looked down, embarrassed. I was surprised that Georgie would ask that question.

Georgie looked at Dr. Khryscoff and then at me. The doctor sipped some red wine, taking his time, giving the question his full attention.

I was surprised that the question was receiving any attention at all.

After thirty seconds or so, Dr. Khryscoff looked at me and said, "That proposal has some interesting possibilities. I am willing to consider it. But there are some things we need to deal with.

"The first hurdle would be getting Chief Petrovic's permission for you to attend the interview. I'm certain you don't want him aware of what you've just told me about your ability. So there needs to be a reason for you to be present. The reason I'll give him is that I would like someone in the room with me as a safety precaution. I have met all his constables and they are all fine and competent policeman, but I feel most comfortable with you.

"The second hurdle would be getting the permission of Henny Mc-Cann. I will talk to her prior to the interview and I think she will be okay with you being there.

"There is one important condition: you will not be able to say anything, or even make any noticeable gesture, unless I request you to. I know this would be impossible for Georgie, but I think you can do it."

When Georgie heard this, she frowned and then giggled.

Dr. Khryscoff continued, "I'll talk to Chief Petrovic first thing tomorrow morning. Then I'll talk to Henny. But I think you can plan on being there with me for Henny's interview."

Thursday, April 27th

CHIEF PETROVIC CALLED his constables together for brief meeting first thing Thursday morning. He informed the constables that late yesterday he had received a call from Henny McCann's lawyer, Fred Donaldson. Mr. Donaldson had told the chief that if he was appointed power of attorney for Henny McCann, he would recommend accepting the terms of the plea bargain.

Mr. Donaldson further explained that Henny McCann did not believe she was guilty of any crime. Consequently, given the opportunity, she would have entered a plea of innocent. Because she was not of sound mind, that was not a realistic plea. A lot depended on Dr. Khryscoff's formal assessment interview of Henny this afternoon.

Chief Petrovic told the group that Dr. Khryscoff had requested that a constable also be present with him at Henny McCann's interview for security reasons. The chief added that Cst. Joel Franklin would be taking on that duty.

DR. KHRYSCOFF AND I were using the supply room again for Henny's interview. The supply room was next door to the Chief's office, but on a different hall than Henny McCann's cell. With the large window and the curtains open, the room was almost pleasant.

Cst. Smith brought Henny to the interview room and remained until she was seated. She seemed quite calm and tentatively smiled at Dr. Khryscoff and me.

Dr. Khryscoff introduced me and asked Henny, "Where would you like Joel to sit?"

"Yes, I know Joel," she said. "He's welcome to sit at the table with us."

"You seem calm today, Henny," said the doctor.

"Yes," said Henny. "I think it's the medication. It keeps me calm but it makes me feel like I'm isolated from everybody. It's almost like there's an invisible wall between me and everything else."

"Are you well enough for the interview?" asked the doctor.

"Yes, I'm glad to get out of my cell," she replied. "I almost hope it's a long interview."

"We do have a little business to take care of before we start," said Dr. Khryscoff. "While you are in jail, we need to appoint someone as your power of attorney so that your business matters can be looked after. For example, you may have bills that have to be paid on your property in Springfield, Illinois; your lawyer will need to be paid; and you might have legal matters to attend to. Do you have any living relatives that could be appointed to do that job?"

"I have no living relatives that I'm aware of," said Henny. "I was married to Dr. Frank McCann for almost four years, but he's deceased and we had no children. I have no idea who I would appoint."

"In cases like this, I always recommend you appoint your lawyer, unless you have a reason not to," said Dr. Khryscoff.

"That makes perfect sense to me," said Henny.

"Just one moment, please," said the doctor. "I'll write down that you wish to grant your lawyer power of attorney. Then I want you to read my note, and, if you're in agreement, sign it."

Dr. Khryscoff wrote a quick note and passed it to Henny. Henny signed the paper and gave it back to the doctor. Dr. Khryscoff had me witness his signature then he folded the paper in half and put it in the back of his notebook.

"Henny, do you know why you are locked up in jail in Chaseford?" Dr. Khryscoff asked.

"I've been told but I don't believe it," Henny responded. "The police say they have signed affidavits stating that I'm Nancy Featherstone. That's not true. I'm Henny McCann. All my identification says I'm Henny McCann.

"They say Nancy Featherstone is under suspicion for murdering her parents. I remember the Featherstones. They were very good to me. I don't remember much about Nancy. Her parents told me she was seldom at the farm. I don't recall ever meeting her."

Henny was starting to get agitated, but at this point she was still in control of herself. This was much different than in her previous interviews. The medication was helping her to remain calm. Dr. Khryscoff was watching her carefully.

"I need to get out of here," she said, suddenly looking uncomfortable. "I feel like I'm losing my mind."

"I only have a couple more questions," said Dr. Khryscoff. "Then you'll be free to leave, Henny."

Henny nodded uncertainly.

"Are you sure you haven't met Nancy Featherstone?" asked the doctor. "She is a dangerous person. She's totally untrustworthy. I think she's evil". The doctor said these sentences without leaving a pause between them for comments.

Henny's eyes suddenly looked a little different to me. I could see rage. But there was no screaming yet.

"I'll ask you again," said Dr. Khryscoff. "Do you know Nancy?"

The woman across the table said, "You stupid fool! I am Nancy!"

"I'm sorry, Nancy. I mistook you for someone else," said the doctor. "Do you know the young gentlemen beside me?"

"I know him," Henny – who was now Nancy – responded. "He's one of the local constables. I don't like any of them. He's one of the guys that came into the interview room when I tried to bite the chief's ear off."

"His name is Joel Franklin," said Dr. Khryscoff. "I'm going to let him ask you some questions. Will you answer them?"

"If I feel like it," Nancy answered.

"Do you remember your mother and father?" I asked.

"I can't forget them," Nancy growled. "They didn't protect me. Everyone who met them thought they were kind and generous people. But when I needed them, they wouldn't listen to me. They wanted almost nothing to do with me. They sent me away to schools and camps whenever they could. If I wanted to do something, they would try to prevent me from doing it.

"When I was small and misbehaved badly, I would be sent to my room. They would lock the door from the outside. When I got older, about 12 or 13, after the bad thing happened to me, they would lock me in the icehouse for an hour. They thought it was funny. They would get a really mean look and say, 'You need to cool off.' They knew I hated the icehouse. Around that time, they told me they would like to have a nice daughter, so they had one ordered from England. That's when Henny came. She wasn't a bad person, but I hated her because my parents really liked her."

"A few minutes ago, you said 'they wouldn't listen to me'. What did you mean by that?" I asked.

"A very bad thing happened to me. I don't like to talk about it. My parents wouldn't let me talk about," said Nancy.

"Dr. Khryscoff and I will listen to you. Tell us about what happened."

Nancy told them the story. "My dad had a really good friend, Alan, who used to come from Toronto to visit us. He came by himself. I don't think he was married. He was very wealthy, so he always brought us gifts. When I was small, he would insist that I sit on his knee. When I got a little older, if I was alone with him, he would touch me where I didn't think he should. I told my mom, but she just said it was my imagination. I learned to stay away from him. That worked till I was 11 years old.

"It was summertime. My dad sent me to the icehouse to get some ice for our kitchen icebox. Alan must've seen me go into the icehouse because he followed me inside and tried to rape me. Maybe he did rape me. I was so scared and confused that I didn't really understand what was happening. I knew he had done a very bad thing, so I went screaming to my parents. They got mad at me and locked me in my room."

Nancy looked distraught. I thought she was going to cry. This certainly was not the Nancy we had dealt with more than once. The Nancy that had uncontrollable lengthy rants. This was not a 'mad' woman.

Dr. Khryscoff and I sat back and quietly waited while Nancy regained her composure. Without being asked, she continued her story.

"After that happened they started sending me away. They sent me to a private school during the fall, winter, and spring. In the summer they sent me to camps. I hated my parents and I didn't trust them to protect me, so I was glad to leave. Alan continued to visit with my family on a regular basis, but I never saw him again because I was at school or at camp. It was about two years after my rape that Henny arrived to become the daughter they wanted."

Dr. Khryscoff said, "Are you able to continue or do you need a break from questioning?" The doctor did not want to stop. They had Nancy present and he didn't want to lose her.

"I'm okay. I'll answer your questions." Nancy said it with a frown, but without shouting.

"Joel, you may continue with the interview," said Dr. Khryscoff.

"Tell us what happened to your mother and father on October 3rd, 1911," I said. "We know there was a fire. We know that your parents were never seen again, and we also know that the body of a young woman was found in the fire."

"I don't want to talk about it," said Nancy. She seemed to have recovered some of her 'not so nice' persona.

"Do you want me to tell you what you did?" I responded.

"I don't think you know. You weren't there. You don't know anything," Nancy said, as if to challenge me.

"I'll give you the short version, Nancy." I looked at her and said, "You had a difficult September. You were using a lot of cocaine. Johnnie Polizzi and Ernie Stanzio came to your parents' farm to pick you up to drive you back to Chicago, so you could return to DePaul University. Your parents refused to let you go. They informed you they were sending you to a sanatorium in the Muskoka region instead. That enraged you. You were already a little paranoid from all the cocaine, and, taking into consideration what you told us earlier in this interview, you had every reason to hate them."

As I talked her pupils grew narrower and narrower. She was becoming very angry. I looked at Dr. Khryscoff. He was busy making notes, but he nodded that I should continue, giving a little downward motion of his hand to say back off a little bit. Before I could continue, Nancy jumped to her feet. She hadn't started screaming but was clearly having difficulty controlling her rage. She started to talk about October 3rd, 1911.

"They were going to send me away again," she shouted. "I'd decided weeks before that I would never be sent away again. The last straw was the arrival of Henny Allenby. She'd rolled up the farm lane and parked in front of our house in her new car the previous evening. They were so happy to see her. I didn't sleep that night. I was far too angry to sleep. Between my anger and the paranoia from the cocaine I was more than irrational. I was murderous.

"My plan was simple: I would poison all three of them and then burn the house to the ground. Then I would take Henny's identification and car and leave. I'd go back to Chicago. I liked it there."

Nancy had become noticeably calmer. She stopped, looked at both of us, and said, "Do you have any other questions?"

I looked at Dr. Khryscoff. He nodded to go ahead.

"Why did you cut your parents up?" I asked.

"I have no idea," she said. "They died so quickly from the poisoning that it made me even angrier. I suppose I didn't think they'd suffered enough. So I cut them up. But I don't really remember. I was out of my mind. I certainly knew that they belonged in the icehouse. That's where they always tried to store me."

"Why did you murder Henrietta Allenby?" I asked.

"She stole my place in the family. She was a constant aggravation and a constant reminder of what my life should have been like."

"Did you murder your husband, Dr. Frank McCann?" I said.

"No, Frank was a good person. He was always nice to me. He helped me get over my addiction."

"Are you Henny or Nancy?" I asked.

Nancy looked at us. She seemed uncertain. "I was quite confused. I started out pretending to be Henny; but as time went on, and my life became pleasant, I really became Henny. I forgot about me. But when I read about the inheritance it upset me. I wasn't sure whether I was Henny or Nancy. You're much better off dealing with Henny than dealing with me."

"I've written down the questions that Joel asked and the answers that you gave," said Dr. Khryscoff. "I would like you to take a few minutes to read it over. When you have finished, if it is accurate, I want you to sign it and date it. Would you do that?"

"I think so. Let me read it first," said Nancy.

Twenty minutes later, Nancy put down the pages of questions and answers that Dr. Khryscoff had given her to read.

"What happens if I sign this?" she asked.

"This statement will be used as your testimony at an inquest into the deaths of your parents," said Dr. Khryscoff. "If you or your power of attorney agrees to the plea bargain that Judge Bernard has proposed, as advised by Chief Petrovic, your lawyer, and I, then there will not be a trial by jury.

"If you enter a plea of guilty to the murder of your parents, then the judge will spare your life. But you will be incarcerated in the secure section of a psychiatric hospital until you are deemed cured. At that time, you will be eligible for parole."

"I don't know what to do," answered Nancy. "If I'm Henny, then I didn't do anything wrong. But I know that as Nancy I committed those murders. But because my parents didn't protect me, I have no remorse for their deaths."

Dr. Khryscoff stood up. He said, "You should talk this over with your lawyer. However, I would like to know who will be talking to the lawyer, you or Henny?"

"I'll do the talking," said Nancy. "It's a matter of life or death."

With that said, Henny McCann was escorted back to her cell. Dr. Khryscoff and I sat in the empty room for a few moments, staring at one another.

"You did really well, Joel," Dr. Khryscoff said finally. "Was she telling the truth? Could you tell?"

"From everything I felt and sensed, Doctor, she told the truth," I replied.

Monday, May 1st

CHIEF PETROVIC WAS in a great mood.

If this meeting wasn't in the police station, thought Cst. Smith, *the chief would probably break out the champagne.*

The body parts mystery had been solved.

Chief Petrovic passed around copies of the statement given by Nancy Featherstone to Dr. Khryscoff and Cst. Franklin.

"I want you to sit at the table and read this through," said the chief. "It will probably take you about twenty minutes or so." Before they had a chance to read it, the chief cautioned them: "You cannot discuss this with anyone else. If you do, it could cost you your job."

When he was sure they'd all read the statement, he collected the copies.

"Life is never as simple as it seems to be," said the chief. "Nancy Featherstone's crimes were atrocious. But it is easy to understand why she was motivated to murder.

"I'm pleased to report that Nancy, or Henny—" The chief paused. "I'll just call her 'the accused'. The accused met with her lawyer Fred Donaldson last Friday afternoon. At that meeting, she agreed to accept the plea bargain that had been proposed by Judge Bernard. There will be no trial by jury. The public will be fully informed about the case at the time of her arraignment. This is a good decision. I congratulate the judge."

Chief Petrovic looked around the table.

"I congratulate all of you. You're all excellent policemen. Without your hard work this case would not have been solved. Thank you very much. The meeting is over."

The Rest of the Story - Friday, August 18th

IT'S FINALLY OVER. Judge Bernard handed the sentence down two days ago, on Wednesday afternoon. It caused a lot of controversy in the community. Many older people, who remembered the Featherstones, were of the opinion 'an eye for an eye'. Hardly any of them remembered Nancy Featherstone. She had rarely been seen in the area after the age of 11.

The local newspaper printed the details of the inquest yesterday. Once the abuse that Nancy Featherstone had been subjected to as a child was revealed, many of the local people understood why the judge had decided to sentence her to imprisonment in a secure psychiatric facility.

Johnnie Polizzi and Ernie Stanzio gave testimony at the inquest. It was important testimony as it connected Nancy Featherstone with the disappearance of Henny Allenby. Dr. Khryscoff had also testified. His testimony was vital in demonstrating that the accused was mentally incapable of making good decisions.

Yesterday's news story has drawn some interest from the big newspapers, especially the Toronto Daily Telegraph and the Chicago Tribune. The reporters are just arriving in town now. They missed the inquest and the judge pronouncing sentence but I'm certain they still have lots of material to work with. I'm sure they have many readers who will be interested to read about a murder involving dismembered body parts and a woman with two distinct personalities.

GEORGIE AND I WERE married on Saturday, June 3rd, to everyone's delight. It was a beautiful day but a little on the hot side. At 2 o'clock it was 93° outside. In the church hall it was closer to 98°. Sylvia was the maid of honour and Jay was the best man. Baby Brad Jarvis, with a lot of help from his grandma, was the ring bearer. As a master of ceremonies, Jay was in his element. There were many toasts. There were many funny anecdotes. Unfortunately, several of the anecdotes presented me as a bumbling young man. I noticed that Georgie applauded wildly at each of these funny stories.

Georgie and I had found a small house to rent, thanks to Gwen Cummings. It was just down the street from Gwen's place. One of her neighbours had just inherited the property.

Dr. Khryscoff and I meet once a month. He visits a few special patients at the 'London Asylum for the Insane' on the second Wednesday and Thursday of every month. Occasionally, he slips up and calls it by that name, then he reminds himself and me that last year the hospital was renamed. It's just called 'Ontario Hospital London', now. That's a much better name.

Dr. Khryscoff always has some small test he wants me to take. I feel like a guinea pig and I probably am one. But he's also talking to me a lot about psychiatric symptoms and identified illnesses, so I'm learning a lot too.

My brother Ralph had a successful tryout with the Cleveland Indians. He received a small signing bonus and is now playing third base in class C ball in the Middle Atlantic League with the Zanesville Grays. My mother wouldn't let him go until he'd finished his final exams. It's a seven-hour drive to Zanesville, Ohio, from Chaseford. Three carloads of us went down to see them play on Saturday July 22nd. We all had a great time, including Ralph, who got two base hits and helped Zanesville win its game.

The end ... for now

About the Author

Many years ago, when I was three, my mother took me to the library. She was delighted that I loved to read. My father was not so happy. He knew books would cut into chore time.

He was right.

I read and I read and I read and I read. Even today I'm reading. And recently I decided to write.

Lightning at 200 Durham Street, and *Where's the Rest of the Body?* are the first two books in the Joel Franklin Mystery series, but there are many more on the way.

Stay tuned.

Made in the USA
Monee, IL
29 July 2021